©SEPTEM

Forward

"The world is ever changing and with this your life may change too, each day is different and every corner has a new beginning, each step takes you further into your journey than you could ever imagine and with every new step life changes with it, embrace the good and the bad, use it to grow and become the person you never thought you could become, life is there for changing, life is there to enjoy and each day writes a new story, stories are to be told, to bring joy to those around you, to inspire others to change their lives and for each and every person in the world to live a wholesome life, as you read this letter your life may be about to change, grasp it with both hands and embark on a journey that will change your life forever, write your own story"

Chapter 1

The days were always slow in Killington, that was until he arrived.

Tumbler was a relatively small guy, round in stature, big brown eyes and long brown hair and looked pretty normal. But there was one thing that really stood out, he always carried a brown leather satchel with the number 7 embossed on the front wherever he went.

No one knew where he came from or what was in his bag.

He just appeared one day and never spoke, he would come into the town around 7am and leave at 7pm every day without fail not really doing anything particular, just walk around.

To the locals he was known as "The oddball"

This continued for a month until one day something weird happened.

It was a Sunday morning and Tumbler was in the town square as normal right on 7am but this time there was something different about him…his bag was missing; his big brown eyes filled with dread and an aura of panic filled the air.

Not many people were around in Killington at 7am but the ones that were would not approach him.

That was until Sledge, the town Bladesmith looked up from stoking his forge and noticed the few people in the square standing around looking at this poor, grief-stricken Oddball.

He left his shop and slowly walked up to Tumbler, placed his massive hand on his shoulder and asked him "What's wrong chap?" Tumbler was taken back as no one had ever spoken to him in the month leading up to this day, but he felt a connection with Sledge that he could not describe and slowly he looked up at Sledge who was a good foot and a half taller than him and said, "They are gone."

"What's gone?" said Sledge in a confused voice, "The Pieces" said Tumbler, his voice trembling with fear.

"What pieces?" "I don't know what you mean, just slow down, take a breath and tell me why these pieces are so important to you!"

Tumbler turned to Sledge and in a reluctant voice said "We can't talk here; can we go somewhere quiet?" so they both walked over to Sledge's workshop and sat on the bench next to the anvil and Tumbler began telling Sledge all about "The Pieces."

"They are called the "Wonder Pieces", when the Great Wall of China was built in 221bc it was found that a part of it had the power to open a doorway to another dimension.

The doorway bought about disasters no one had ever seen or ever spoken about but one of the builders noticed that a part of the wall was glowing green, he removed the green piece and the doorway closed, the piece was kept in a secure

location that only he knew about and the disasters stopped"
Sledge looked at him in disbelief but allowed Tumbler to
continue his story.

"Then one day an old man was walking past the entrance to
Petra in Egypt and noticed a green glow coming from the
inside of the structure, he was drawn in by an unusual
humming and saw a green piece above a doorway and as he
slowly approached the opening the ground started to shake,
he lost his balance, reached out and grabbed hold of the
green piece above the door and it came away in his hand, the
shaking stopped, he got to his feet and ran back to his town
with the piece in his hand, he found a wiseman who
happened to know about the events surrounding the piece
found by the builder of the Great wall and took it from the
man and as the other 4 Great wonders were searched they
were all found to have the same small green piece, so they
were taken, stored together and hidden from the world and
"The Protectors of the Septem" was formed.

"Septem?" said Sledge intrigued but for some reason
Tumbler did not answer, he just sat there staring at the sky.

"Are they what you carry in that bag with the seven on the
front? And why do you have them," said Sledge.

"Yes" said Tumbler "And the reason I have them is because I
am the current Protector of the Septem and have been since
my Father and his Great grandfather before him, it was my
Great Grandfather Asim that started the Protectors of the
Septem, and they have been in our safe keeping for
generations until today when I woke and the bag was gone".

"There's that word again! Septem! What is it?" but again Tumbler just said nothing.

"But hang on a minute" said Sledge a little confused "If 1 came from the Great Wall, the other from Petra that's two and you said the other four were searched that's only six, so why are there 7 Pieces in the bag and only six wonders" Sledge was puzzled.

"There are 7 pieces but only 6 of the glowed green, the last didn't start glowing until the New 7 wonders where officially announced in 2007 and that's because the 7th is the most recent, Christ the Redeemer in Rio de Janeiro, Brazil, it wasn't completed until 1931 so the 7th Piece stayed dormant until then, I am the first Protector of the Septem to know all 7 destinations".

"But who would want to steal your bag? No one knows who you are!" said Sledge confused.

"The only person I can think of is Annakus, she has been searching for the Pieces for years, which is why I move around so much, she must have found me and taken the bag, we need to stop her before she puts all the pieces back" Tumbler was trembling, and the only thing Sledge could think about was that he had so many questions.

"But what happens if all the Pieces are put back?" said Sledge sitting on the edge of the bench getting even closer to Tumbler with each word, "And why are they so important?" still not sure whether to believe him.

"They are important because as each piece is put back into its rightful place in each of the 7 wonders of the world it will give it the power it needs to open the doorway and allow a creature of awesome power to enter our dimension and cause havoc, but if it's put back earlier it will trigger a small disaster that is meant to act as a distraction until the time comes for the doorway to open and if that happens then who knows, we must find those pieces!"

"But what happens if all 7 pieces are put back" said Sledge with a little fear in his voice, Tumbler looked right at Sledge, his big brown eyes widened even more, sweat running down his forehead and he just sighed.

After what seemed like an eternity Sledge turned to Tumbler and in a determined voice said, "Where do we start looking?"

Astonished Tumbler looked at him and said "You want to help me? Why?" Sledge stood up "Well someone has to; you can't do it on your own!"

"Well, the pieces need to be put back in order for the Septem to open so the first piece was the from The Great Wall, So I guess we start in China," said Tumbler.

Chapter 2

Sledge pulled a bag out of a large chest that sat underneath his work bench and started packing essential item, although he did not really know what he should be taking and how long he was going to be gone for.

He was born in Killington a small town in the highlands of Scotland, tucked away off the beaten track and not many people knew it was even there, he grew up there and loved it, he had never left, never travelled and this is where he learnt his trade as a Bladesmith from his father.

Sledge was a big guy, 6ft 11 and towered above Tumblers 5ft 4 frame, he had hands like shovels, long red hair and a long red beard that he had plaited to keep as much of it away from the forge as possible but it still had a few singed hairs that were curled up on the ends, his eyes were blue and looked like 2 sapphires had been implanted in his head, his nose was relatively large but in proportion with his face which was weathered with years of working in the atmosphere of the smoky, dirty workshop, Tumbler was glad he was going with him, he felt safe for the first time in years.

"Sledge, that's not a very Scottish name" Tumbler said to him as the Scotsman packed yet another knife into his bag.

"That was not always my name" replied Sledge.

"My real name is Dougal ...doesn't really have that right ring to it does it, Dougal the Bladesmith" Sledge had a little grin on his face and Tumbler was not sure whether to grin back so he just stared at the first thing he saw in the room, a broad axe, Sledge was quite an intimidating character but Tumbler felt a warmth come from him when he smiled and this was the first time he had seen him smile.

"So why Sledge?" Tumbler enquired.

"My father was a big guy like me, looked like a bear, he had a deep booming voice and whilst he was forging the steel to make his next blade I used to sit on that upturned barrel in the corner" he pointed to an old Whiskey barrel in the corner of the workshop "I'd just watch my father making a lot of the weapons you see around you, once the steel was hot enough he used to have a Sledge hammer with half the handle cut off that he used to hammer out the steel, he always used to shout "bring me the Sledge or pass the Sledge" "It became our thing and my father nicknamed me Sledge and that's how it stuck, you're the first person to know my real name in years"

Tumbler felt good about this, Sledge trusted him, and he trusted Sledge and with the journey ahead that is what they both needed...Trust.

The workshop was full of an array of weapons, Swords, knives, Axes, daggers, you name it they were there just hanging from every available space, Sledge picked up a dagger from the anvil and put it in his bag, It shone in the sunlight that broke through a small hole in the roof of the workshop "What's that?" said Tumbler still looking around the workshop in oar, "It's called a Dirk, it was used by Officers in the Scottish highlands regiment around the 1800s and is the first dagger my father taught me to make back when I was only 9 years old, this dagger is 31 years old and never been used and let's hope it stays that way" There was a hint of optimism in his voice that was quickly overcome by doubt but neither of them knew what they would face.

"What's it made of" enquired Tumbler, fascinated by its mirror like blade and shining handle.

"The blade is made out of 150-layer ladder Damascus steel and the handle is made from silver" replied Sledge pushing the blade into its sheath and throwing it in the bag.

Five minutes past with neither of them saying anything whilst Sledge packed the last few things into his bag, as he put the last pair of thick woolly socks into the side pocket of the bag along with his passport that Tumbler thought was odd for someone who had never travelled outside of Killington to have a passport but just brushed it over and didn't ask, he turned to Tumbler, "All I know about you is that you are the Protector of the Septem, which I still don't know what that is by the way" hoping to get a reaction from Tumbler when he mentioned Septem again for what seemed like the hundredth time but nothing stirred, Sledge paused for a minute but still nothing so he left it.

Chapter 3

"There isn't much to say really" acknowledged Tumbler "I don't have anywhere that I call home as such although my father, Grandmother and Great Grandfather were from Egypt I am not really sure where I was born as my mother died during child birth and my father never spoke about her, he was so committed to the Protectors of the Septem that's all he spoke about, I guess to get me ready for when it was my turn, he always told me if I don't know too much about my past then my enemies don't have anything on me, that is one of the reasons we had to move around so much and is why I never settle in anywhere for too long, to keep one step ahead of the people who want to get what I possess, what I protect however Annakus caught up with me didn't she and now look what's happened, I let my father down" Tumbler had a crackle in his voice, like he was about to cry but he held it back and carried on talking.

"You haven't let him down, you have done your best and that's all you can ask for" Sledge put his shovel like hand on Tumbler's shoulder and squeezed it sympathetically, Tumbler grimaced a little, it felt like his shoulder had been put into a vice, but it was reassuring to him.

"How long have you been the Protector of the Septem?" asked Sledge grabbing a jug full of what looked like Ale and having a massive swig, "Want some?"

"No thanks" replied Tumbler "I don't drink, I have to keep my head clear."

"OK I'll have your share" grinned Sledge and took another big gulp out of the jug.

"I've lost count now" Tumbler looked into the air as if he was counting in his head, after a few minutes Tumbler looked straight at Sledge and said "157 years", Sledge almost dropped the jug but managed to catch it just before it hit the floor only spilling a small amount of the ale that was left.

"157 years" he spluttered "How old are you?".

"I'm 172", The room went quiet, Sledge was not sure how to react to this, the guy only looked in his mid-30s…" You were born in 1849!" Sledge was astonished.

"Yep" Tumbler said casually "I became Protector of the Septem when I was fifteen, I remember the day it happened, you might as well sit down for a bit" Tumbler gestured towards the upturned whiskey barrel, Sledge sat down, and Tumbler began.

"It was January 15th 1864, we were in America during the American Civil war, we had come across a troop of Union soldiers lead by General William Sherman, one of the soldiers spotted us and we hid behind a bush, we could hear him coming closer when all of a sudden I heard my father call out, the soldier had put his hand on my father's back and he must of jumped 6ft in the air, I remember grinning but he didn't find it funny, the soldier took us to General Sherman who said "Where are you two going, what are you doing here and are you Confederates?" "He fired lots of questions at us in a brief period of time, but my father just kept the answers short and sweet."

"Nowhere particular and no we are not confederates, we have travelled to the Americas from Europe" my father said, "What is in the bag?" enquired Sherman, "My father just looked at him and said "Rocks, my son collects rocks" "I looked at my father with a confused look on my face and my father just looked back at me and gave a subtle shake of his head like he was saying "just go with it".

Sledge now had his elbows on his knees and his head resting in his hands listening inventively to Tumbler, Tumbler continued telling his story.

"General Sherman then said to us "We are marching South, and you are more than welcome to join us but be on your toes, anything could be up head, we are setting up camp now so we will get you fed and watered and be on our way in the morning."

"My father and I thanked him, and we laid out on the floor staring at the stars relaxing after filling our bellies" Tumbler had a look of someone who was living the moment again and had the smallest of grins on his face, he sighed.

"Now I don't know how well you know your American Civil war history" Tumbler directed at Sledge, Sledge shrugged his shoulder as if to say "not much" so Tumbler continued "It was the following day 16th January 1864, we had marched with the union troops to just outside Dandridge, Tennessee when all of a sudden the air was filled with the sound of musket fire, the Union troops scattered and Confederate Soldiers lead by General James Longstreet appeared from nowhere, my father pushed me to the ground and laid on top of me, the noise was deafening, people were screaming and I managed to lift my head far enough off the ground to see bodies dropping all over the place, we laid there for what felt like eternity and then my father grabbed my shirt, gave me the bag with the Pieces in and told me to run for cover, I just got up and ran as fast as I could, when I looked back I couldn't see him, he was gone, I stopped for a moment and thought about carrying on and maybe he would catch up or should I go back, I went back and there he was lying on his back with blood coming out of the corner of his mouth, he had taken a musket shot directly to his stomach and one in his left shoulder, I fell to my knees and cradled his head, his eyes were barely open, he managed to open one eye and the words that come out of his mouth that day will stay with me for the rest of my life, he said "It's your time now, remember what I've taught you, keep moving, remember Gi" I then remember a gurgle, he squeezed my hand and he was gone, I remember asking him who Gi was but it was too late", Tumblers eyes welled up and a single tear ran down his face "That's when I knew the Pieces were my responsibility, I was the new Protector of the Septem and I had to keep moving as he had said and for the last 157 years that's what I have done"

"Wow" this was the only word Sledge could find in his vocabulary at that moment in time that could express what he was feeling, "So for the last 157 years it has just been you?" "Yes," replied Tumbler, like my father told me, keep moving, I haven't been anywhere long enough to make friends or meet people and today is the first time I have had a full-blown conversation with anyone but now I have put your life in danger" he looked at the floor in disappointment.

"Hey, look at me, look around you" Sledge shouted at Tumbler "I can look after myself, I'm not scared and whatever we are about to face will have to think twice before it decides to take on me."

Tumbler stood up suddenly as if someone had just taken him by surprise and said in a confident, loud voice "Well have you finished packing and drinking, we better go, Annakus could have already put the first Piece back in the Great wall and China could be in danger, so no more stories, grab your gear and let's move!"

Sledge was a little taken back by this sudden change in character, but he liked it "OK boss" he said sarcastically "let's go."

They grabbed their things and walked out of the workshop to the outskirts of the town, Sledge looked at the sign that said "Thank you for driving carefully through Killington" took a deep breath and off they went, destined for China.

Chapter 4

It had been a long flight, especially for Sledge who in his 40 years on the planet had never been on any form of public transport and had now just completed just over 10 hours on an aeroplane, had safely landed at Beijing Capital International Airport.

The large clock on the wall showed 8:04am Friday 1st May, and the temperature was around 18 degrees, Tumbler and Sledge stood outside the airport, Sledge had his bag in one hand and a deep-fried Dough stick in the other, Tumbler looked at him funny and said, "That normally comes with Soya bean milk, your meant to dip the dough stick in the milk!" Sledge had a look of disgust on his face "I threw that away it tasted awful, anyway remember I'm from Scotland, anything that says "Deep Fried" is good for me" the look on his face turned from disgust to laughter, Tumbler just shook his head and began thinking.

"So, what do we do from here?" Sledge asked Tumbler.

"Well, we need to get to the Great Wall as quickly as possible, apparently it is about 60 kilometres from here to Mutianyu which is the closest part of the wall to Beijing airport and then" but before Tumbler could finish talking Sledge looked at him in surprise "Apparently! what do you mean apparently, I thought you had been here before?

"What made you think that?" said Tumbler.

"Well, you're the Protector of the Septem, I thought in the 157 years that you had been protecting the pieces you would have at least visited the 7 Wonders of the World, see where they had come from!" Sledge's voice was filled with an air of annoyance and confusion.

Tumbler looked at Sledge, "My father told me to never visit the locations of the Wonders, I was to keep the pieces away from their original locations as it was too risky for them to be too close, so I've always travelled to remote locations around the globe, which is why I choose Killington, small town in Scotland I thought no one would find me there".

"But they did, who is this Annakus anyway? Sledge enquired.

"I'll tell you on the way," Tumbler got into a Taxi, Sledge threw his bag in back seat with him and joined the driver in the front and they set off.

10 minutes into the journey Sledge asked again "So who is this Annakus?"

"She was my Great Grandfather Asim's assistant back in 1680, he was a wiseman back in Egypt and people came from miles around to hear his stories about the Wonder Pieces, but to them they were only stories, they didn't know the truth, only he knew they actually existed, he was the Protector at the time, Annakus had heard the stories many times and the more she heard the more she wanted to know if they were real, Asim just brushed it over and told her they were just stories" he paused for a minute, "Now I think of it Asim actually means Protector in Egyptian, huh what a coincidence".

He continued with his story, "Then one day Annakus was alone and she sneaked into his study and found that the desk had moved, she went to push it back and noticed a breeze coming up from a gap in the floor, she pushed the desk back further which revealed a small staircase, she walked down the steps into a room, it had 7 sides and 6 of the walls had a painting on each of the 6 locations of the glowing green pieces and the 7th wall was blank, they were laid out on the walls in order from oldest to newest and in the middle of the room was a chest, she slowly opened the chest and inside was the Satchel with the 7 on the front" Tumbler paused.

"The one you were carrying?" Sledge asked.

"Yes, she took the bag out of the chest and opened it and that's when she saw the Wonder Pieces for the first time, 6 glowing green and 1 not glowing at all, The Mystery Piece, but what she didn't realise that my Asim was stood at the bottom of the steps, she dropped the bag and they just looked at each other, my Great Grandfather pulled her out of the room and made her leave, he had trusted her and the trust was gone and the following day she returned only to find that the house was empty, the desk was pulled back and the room was empty, he had left during the night and taken everything, she never saw him or the bag again and has been searching for the bag ever since, Annakus left a different person that day, she had felt a power that she had never felt before and wanted it for herself, she became obsessed but the Protectors of the Septem kept one step ahead"

"But why did Asim keep her so close for so long?" Sledge asked intrigued.

"She was his daughter!" Tumbler replied, Sledge's jaw dropped "His daughter?" Sledge said astounded "Your Fathers mother?"

"No, Asim had 2 daughters, Annakus and Joshinda, Annakus never had children, she was too busy trying to track down the Pieces to have children, Joshinda is my father's mother, the title of Protector of the Septem is only passed on to the males of the family, it is tradition, so Asim trained my father who in turn trained me".

"I wish I had never asked now" Sledge replied "But why now? Why would she travel all the way to China to put the Piece back? What has she got to achieve?

"Well you remember back in Killington when I told you that the New 7 Wonders of the World weren't officially announced until 2007 and Christ the Redeemer was the newest as it was only completed in 1931, 2007 was the year the Mystery seventh Piece started glowing, that's why the seventh wall in the room with the bag in was blank, my Grandfather knew there were 7 doorways, he had the 7 pieces but didn't know where the seventh Piece had to go, he just knew that he had to protect them all to protect the Septem, she must of worked it out, you think about it, she has had years of searching and in all those years she has been wondering why the seventh piece wasn't glowing, she has been tracking me all this time and nearly 14 years after the official announcement she finally found me and the bag and now the true power of the Septem can be released" Tumbler was in a real panic now.

"What have I let myself in for?" Sledge asked himself, he asked himself the question in his head as to not worry Tumbler even more.

Tumbler thought for a while and on the floor of the taxi was a flyer, it was advertising a festival, he read it out to Sledge "The Great Wall festival, 1st – 3rd of May" What's that?" asked Sledge, Tumbler looked at him "It's a 30 hour techno party that is held in the shadow of the Great Wall in the Beijing Huaibei Ski resort, some of the biggest names in Techno will be there along with thousands of people" he dropped the flyer, "She is going to open the first doorway, we need to get to the part of the wall the piece came from before she puts it back or shit is going to hit the fan!" This was the first time Sledge had heard Tumbler swear but under the circumstances he let him off and just as he was about to ask another question the taxi pulled up beside the road and they both got out.

Chapter 5

"They both stared at the massive structure in front of them and started walking, after what seemed like hours, they felt a distant rumble and a flash of green in the distance, "That can't be good can it" asked Sledge, Tumbler had stopped dead "She is here, oh my god she has done it" "What has she done?" asked Sledge and then it dawned on him "She has put the piece back hasn't she?

"It's a possibility or she just may be close" he had the sound of dread in his voice, "We need to get to the Mutianyu section of the wall, it's the part that used to serve as the northern barrier defending the capital and the imperial tombs, this is where the piece came from, this is where she will be headed if she isn't there already!"

As they made their way closer to the source of the green light the rumbling got louder and louder and large parts of the wall were shaking making it hard to walk, then suddenly up ahead Tumbler saw a figure holding a glowing green object in its outreached hand, "It's her!" he said and as he said that the figure looked right at him and forced the piece into a gap in the wall.

The whole wall shuddered, the sky went dark and the noise was deafening, both Tumbler and Sledge put their hands over their ears as tight as they could and dropped to their knees, Tumbler managed to look up for a split second and saw her, it was Annakus, her long black hair and dark eyes were unmistakable and she wore a long black dress, her skin was tanned and her face gaunt, he knew it was her from the picture his father had shown him and she hadn't changed a bit from that photo he had seen back in 1864.

They both stood up, clearly shaken by what was happening around them and the first thing they noticed was Annakus was gone, she had just vanished.

"We need to get there and pull it out" said Sledge with both panic and shock in his voice.

"It's not that easy" Said Tumbler "Once the Piece is in, the doorway opens in whatever location the holder of the Piece wants it to and whatever is lurking behind the doorway is unleashed, the only choice we have is to get to the festival."

"What is going to come out of that doorway?" panic covered Sledges weathered face.

"You will know when you see it said Tumbler, "let's go."

They jumped into the first taxi they came across, Tumbler waved the flyer I the drivers face and with a raised voice shouted, "Take us here, quick!"

The taxi driver flicked on the meter and off they sped to the Great wall festival.

When they finally arrived, Tumbler paid the fare and they rushed into the resort, they stood out like a sore thumb amongst the thousands of Techno trolls all covered in their fluorescent body paints and waving their glow sticks, Tumbler was dressed in what could only be described as something a vagrant would wear, baggy brown trousers, a shirt that looked 2 sizes too big for him and a leather peaked cap and Sledge wearing a leather waistcoat, black trousers and big black leather boots looked like he had just walked out of a heavy metal concert, they were blinded by the array of multi coloured lasers that darted around the venue and the music was so loud Sledge felt like he had two hearts beating in his chest

They scanned the bouncing crowd to see if they could spot Annakus but she was nowhere to be seen, they barged past people waving their glow sticks in the air and Sledge towered above the Chinese party goers by a good foot or more however Tumbler was having to take steps and then a little hop to see above the crowd, after around 20 minutes of looking they couldn't see her but then they felt it, a shaking that was nothing to do with the music, a rumble that sounded like thunder, the lasers went off and in the distance was a bright light, thousands of people turned and cheered, throwing their fists in the air as if the DJ was about to do something amazing but it wasn't part of the show, out of the light came a dragon, it was massive, its head was just like you would see in Chinese festival parades, typical dragon like, its body was long like a serpent and it had 5 claws on each foot that were at least 12 inches long just like the Dirk Dagger Sledge had packed in his bag back in Killington, the dragon was a deep green with red spines running from the top of its head to the base of its tale which was swinging in all directions and it was roaring so loud it sounded like a pack of lions were in its mouth roaring for it.

Sledge looked in disbelief "What the hell is that?" he looked at Tumbler who stood right in front of him with his mouth open so wide his jaw could have touched the floor.

"That's Shenlong!" Tumbler replied with his mouth still wide open, "it is known in Chinese myths to be the Master of Storms and the bringer of rain".

The crowd were still cheering and punching the air in the direction of the DJ who was looking back at them with a confused look as if to say, "That's not me doing that!" and that's when the sky turned black, clouds filled the space above the festival and the Thunder started rolling, lightning was striking everything, speaker were blowing and sparks were flying everywhere, that's when the party goers knew this wasn't part of the act, their faces turned from euphoria to sheer fright, people were scattering all over the place and this riled Shenlong, it crashed through the people and brightly coloured bodies were flying all over the place, people were screaming and writhing on the floor in pain from wounds caused by Shenlong's claws and thrashing tail.

As Shenlong got angrier the storm got worse and the rain was so hard that you could only just see your hand in front of your face, the ground was starting to flood which did not help the frightened crowd so now people were slipping in the mud and getting trampled, it was madness.

"We need to stop this and now" said Sledge with urgency in his voice and before Tumbler could reply he was gone.

Time seemed to be going in slow motion for Tumbler and eventually out of the crowd he saw Sledge, Dagger in his hand running as fast as his 6ft 11 frame would let him and for a man his size leapt a good six foot onto the trashing tale of Shenlong.

He held on with all his strength, he started to slip so he plunged the dagger into Shenlong's tail and reached for his boot, he pulled out a second smaller knife and just like a mountaineer scaling a mountain face he plunged knife, dagger, knife, dagger between the scales and made his way towards the top of its head, he was almost there when the knife missed the fleshy space and hit one of the scales bouncing off as if he was trying to pierce metal with a tooth pick, he hung on to the dagger handle with one hand and was swung around like a rag doll.

Tumbler gasped and reached for his pocket and pulled out a pebble the size of a marble, he ran as fast as his legs could carry him and just as he was in reaching distance of Shenlong's head he threw the marble as hard as he could, it made contact with Shenlong's snout and there was an almighty explosions, Sledge still hanging on with one hand was thrown up in the air and came down with a crash half way down its back, he plunged the knife and dagger between the scales just in time as the dragon started thrashing around, rubbing its snout into the dirt, its front legs gave out from under it which gave Sledge the time he needed to reach its head and with one swift slice of the dagger cut Shenlong's throat, it let out one final blood curdling roar and its back legs gave out too and came crashing to the floor.

They both slumped to the floor and gasped for air, their lungs filled with oxygen "My god that was intense!" said Sledge between breaths.

They looked around at all the bodies, some not moving at all, some sitting against upturned speaker or collapsed lighting rigs, people were helping others, and some were even taking selfies next to the fallen Shenlong, Tumbler and Sledge just looked at each other, shook their heads and at the same time said, "Some people!"

They got up from their resting place and Sledge pulled his knife out of the dragon's neck, wiped it off on is shirt sleeve and pushed it back into his boot.

Tumbler looked up at the stage and there she was, Annakus was standing there with the biggest of grins on her face, her hands clasped together in joy at the carnage she had created and the pain she had caused, before Tumbler could get Sledge's attention, she turned her back on him and vanished into thin air.

"She was here" he shouted at Sledge who was wiping the congealed blood off the blade of his dagger.

"Well, where is she now?" Sledge shouted back.

"She's gone, she just vanished!"

Sledge walked up to Tumbler and knelt so he would be face to face with him.

"How does she just keep vanishing like that?"

"She must possess an Iter stone" replied Tumbler confused.

"What on earth is an Iter stone?" said Sledge baffled at the thought of learning something else he did not really want to know.

"Iter is Latin for Journey, whoever possess an Iter stone has the ability to travel through time in an instant" but before he could continue Sledge stood bolt upright and in an annoyed voice said, "Do you have one?", "Yep, all the Protectors of the Septem get 2, one for back up and another to use when the other is regenerating" replied Tumbler casually pulling it out of his other pocket.

Even more annoyed now Sledge turned his back and said, "So you made me travel all this way on that damn airplane, over 10 hours for my first ever flight and you could off just zap us here from Scotland?" he was now a good ten foot away from Tumbler, kicking one of the broken speakers as hard as he could.

"No, the Iter Stones only allows 1 person to travel at a time and take 3 hours to re-charge after each use due to the amount of power it uses" then he realised how she got it.

"I kept one in my pocket at all times and the other in the bag with the Wonder Pieces, I forgot all about it until now."

"So, she could already be at the second destination, what if we are too late?" Sledge had calmed down a little now but there was a hint of panic in his voice.

"She could be, yes, but once one doorway is opened the next cannot be opened for 24hrs, the next location senses a Piece has been used and puts a time lock on as a safety protocol, Annakus knows this so we should be able to reach the second location with enough time to stop her.

"So where is the next location?" Sledge said with a sigh.

"Petra, Egypt" "If we leave now, get to the airport, catch a plane to King Hussein international airport which is the closest to Petra, the flight takes just over 9hrs so it should give us a good 12 hours to track down Annakus and hopefully stop her before she can put the next Wonder Piece back, we better go now, I don't fancy having to try and explain to the Chinese authorities why there is a mythical dragon lying dead in the middle of a Techno festival, they can't really blame it on a drug hallucination can they" Tumbler smirked but all Sledge could think about was he had never travelled in his life and he was just about to get onto his second aeroplane in the space of less than 12 hrs, he grabbed his bag, hailed a taxi and they both made their way to Beijing International airport destined for Egypt.

Chapter 6

It was 10am on Friday 1st May when they landed at King Hussein International airport in Jordan, this confused Sledge due to them landing in China at 8am on the same day until Tumbler explained that due to the time difference Egypt is 6 hours behind China, no wonder he felt odd, this was a new experience for him, the outside temperature was already peaking 25.C and the dry air hit Sledge in the face as soon as he stepped off the plane like someone pointing a hair dryer at him, the airport was surrounded by huge sand-coloured mountains that seemed to go on forever and the sky was a beautiful blue.

They walked across the runway toward the baggage collection and waiting for Sledges bag to be unloaded, as usual this took an age but eventually they both saw it slowly moving its way towards them on the conveyor, as they walked towards the exit Tumbler turned to see Sledge had stopped at a Food kiosk, Tumbler couldn't hear what he was ordering but as he got closer he could see what it was, Sledge was scoffing down Falafel, "I spotted the words Deep and

Fried again and thought why not try it, I'm in a new country, why not see what other countries deep fry" he smiled at Tumbler who just grinned back "What do you think?" he said back, "Meh, its ok I suppose" said Sledge not overly impressed but he swallowed anyway.

They stood in the dry air outside the airport gazing at the mountains in front of them, people were rushing through the doors to catch their plane or rushing to taxis parked waiting for their next fare, there was a lot going on.

Tumbler walked up to the open driver's window of the first available taxi he could find "How long does it take to get to Petra from here" he asked, the driver flicked his half-smoked cigarette onto the floor just missing Tumbler's shoe and replied, "Just under 2hrs my friend, but why the rush? why not stop at South beach, do some snorkelling, get a tan on that chalky white skin".

"We're fine, we want to go straight to Petra, can you take us?" said Tumbler looking at his white arms and seeing Sledge doing the same.

"Jump in, throw the bag in the trunk", "I'll hold onto it if that's alright with you" acknowledged Sledge, he did not want anyone else accidently getting their hands on the multitude of knives he had tucked away in every available compartment, he got in the back on put the bag on the floor by his feet, Tumbler got in next to him and off they went.

"What you are doing in Petra, bit of sight-seeing?" the driver asked trying to make the normal taxi driver conversation, they looked at each other for a minute and Tumbler looked to the front of the car and could see the drivers ID swinging from the rear-view mirror "Amun is it?" Tumbler enquired "Yes, it is sir" replied Amun "It means God of Mystery, maybe my parents knew I would be a taxi driver and thought everyday my job would be a mystery, you met all sorts of people in this job and it's a mystery where they will be going until you ask."

"Well, Amun" Tumbler continued, "I suppose you could say we are sight-seeing we just don't know what we expect to see yet."

"That is a mystery" replied Amun but quickly worked out he was not going to get much information from this fare so lit up another cigarette and turned on the radio.

Half an hour past and it was getting hot in the back of the taxi, sweat was staring to drip down Sledges forehead, he tied his long red hair into a man bun, Tumbler looked at him and smirked "What?" said Sledge fumbling with a hair band, "you try dealing with this heat with all the hair I have on my face", he wiped his forehead with a dirty handkerchief he pulled out of his waistcoat pocket and wound down the window but the air blowing through did not help, he wound it back up and asked Amun to crank up the air con, "Its up as far as it will go my friend!" said Amun so Sledge just left it and slumped down in the seat.

Another 20 minutes past and the taxi pulled up to a stop on the side of the road in the centre of Wadi Musa "That will be 85JD my friend" Tumbler looked at Sledge, there was silence for a minute then Sledge sighed, pulled out 100 and said, "Keep the change and get the air con fixed" Amun looked at him strangely, took the money and drove off into the distance.

They stood side by side, looking around for somewhere to grab a drink and across the road they saw a small kiosk, they ran over to it and ordered two bottles of water and gulped them down like they hadn't drank for days, Sledge wiped his forehead again and Tumbler enquired with the kiosk owner which direction they needed to go to reach Petra, the guy pointed over Tumblers shoulder, he thanked him and turned to Sledge who was sitting on the sandy ground, head resting on his knees.

As Tumbler was walking back to where his travel companion was sitting, the soggy, sweaty rag dripping on the floor in front of him he felt like he was being watched, he stopped and turned, looking back at the kiosk he had just left but no one was there, just the kiosk owner waving back at him, he carried on walking and he felt it again, like someone was watching his every move, he kept walking and suddenly spun round on his feet hoping that he would turn quick enough to see someone there but he was too slow, he didn't catch the face but he did see what looked like part of a purple and green kaftan disappear around the back of the kiosk he had just been too, his eyes narrowed for a moment, trying to search the deep dark corners of his memory to see if anything jumped out but nothing did, he finally got back to Sledge who looked up at him with his tired eyes "What were you looking at back there?", Tumbler was still thinking but managed to respond "I'm not sure, it felt like I was being followed but", he paused for a moment "Nah its ok, it must be nothing".

"Maybe its Annakus" replied Sledge wiping his brow for a third time.

"No, I don't think so, let's just forget about it, probably just the haze playing tricks on my eyes" Tumbler just brushed it off and continued to tell Sledge what the Kiosk owner had said.

"It's about 20 minutes this way to the entrance of Petra", Sledge rose to his feet and said, "let's make a move then, maybe we might find a bit of shade there" Tumbler raised his eyebrows and started walking.

Tumbler had one last look over his shoulder at the kiosk again just in case, but it was normal, so he continued walking.

5 minutes into their walk they passed a guide who was holding the reins of two camels, both saddled up ready to go, the guide beckoned them over ""20 Egyptian Pounds, my friend's, only 20 Egyptian Pounds, very cheap".

"Each?" said Sedge in a shocked voice "To ride a big horse with a hump, no thanks I'll walk."

"Yes each, but you will get there quicker, you look very hot" the guide said with persuasion in his voice.

Tumbler stopped, turned to the guide and asked, "What do you know about Petra?"

"I know a lot sir, I have been giving these tours for years, holiday makers love it when I mention Indiana Jones and the Last Crusade, they ask me if there really was a knight in Al-Khazneh temple, I tell them I don't know as I cannot get past the blades, silly tourists" he smiles at them and laughs out loud.

Tumblers looks at him for a minute not sure whether to laugh or not, after he while he says, "I'll pay you 30 Egyptian pounds for both and you lead us to Al-Khazneh" "35" says the guide, "30 or I find another guide" Tumblers replies "OK, 30 but I only take you there I do not bring you back" says the guide, "Deal" replies Tumbler "What is your name?" "My name is Bes" said the guide, "it means "Brings joy."

"OK Bes let's get on these Camels and go, we need to get there quick" there was urgency in Tumbler's voice now and Sledge agreed as the temperature was rising and so was his temperature.

Bes helped them both onto the camels and started leading them by the reins across the sands toward Petra.

"What is Al-Khazneh? Sledge asked Bes.

Bes replied "Al-Khazneh is one of the most elaborate temples in Petra, it was inhabited by the Arabs in ancient times and like the other buildings including the monastery are all carved directly into the sandstone rock face, it is beautiful especially at night."

"What is inside the temple?" ask Sledge, "Nothing, just an empty chamber, there is nothing of any importance inside, not like they show in Indiana Jones" replied Bes.

"I beg to differ" Tumbler said under his breath, "What said Bes, "Oh nothing" replied Tumbler looking at Sledge with raised eyebrows, Sledge made a gesture as if he was zipping his mouth closed and then there was silence.

Chapter 7

They arrived at the entrance to Al-Khazneh temple at just at 11:30am, the camels lowered themselves to the ground and the two jumped off, Bes took the 30 off Tumbler and turned to make his way back to the centre of Wadi Musa, "Thank you" shouted Tumbler, Bes turned "Take lots of photos" and off he went with the camels in tow.

They waited for Bes to be far enough away, and they walked through the crowds of people already taking photos and moved as close as they could to the entrance of the Temple, when they thought no one was looking they rushed through to doorway into the empty chamber, the only light in there was the sunlight and Tumbler was looking around the walls looking for the shape of the Wonder Piece.

"Has Annakus been here yet?" asked Sledge.

"No, firstly there is no green light only sunlight and secondly there is no mythical beast causing a scene and killing the tourists" replied Tumbler with a little sarcasm in his voice ".

"How far up are we looking" said Sledge trying to help as much as he could.

"It can't be that far up, remember me telling you that the man who found the piece fell when the floor rumbled and he grabbed it to stop himself falling, well that means it's at arm's reach so it must be here somewhere."

After a lot of staring into nothingness, he saw it, the space where the Piece should be, "What do we do now" said Sledge "We wait" replied Tumbler, so they found a dark corner, sat down, and waited.

Hours past and Sledge had nodded off, head resting on his bag when all of a sudden Tumbler saw a figure moving towards the doorway of the temple, he squinted and in the shadow of the doorway he saw the outline of a satchel draped across her chest, he squinted again then he saw the 7, it was her, Annakus was there, Tumbler nudged Sledge and before Sledge could say anything Tumbler has pushed his hand over his mouth and as silently as he could said "Sshh".

Annakus was looking at her watch, she opened the bag and the chamber filled with green light, she took out the Wonder Piece and pushed it into the space in the wall, nothing happened, the light of the Piece faded to a subtle glow and there was silence.

"What happened?" Sledge whispered to Tumbler confused.

"It's not time yet, remember I said back in China that once one doorway is opened the next cannot be opened for 24hrs, the next location senses a Piece has been used and puts a time lock on as a safety protocol, she must have mis-judged the time".

"Because of the time difference I guess!" said Sledge pleased with himself.

"No, The Pieces don't follow the rules of time zones, they just know in one location it was 4pm so to them 24hrs later is 4pm too, it just triggers a 24-hour countdown, so its 3:50pm now, we have 10 minutes" Tumbler looked at is watch to double check, 3:51pm, 9 minutes.

"Let's take her out then and grab the Pieces" Sledge said ready to lunge out of the darkness and before Tumbler could stop him he was gone, Tumbler saw the large shadowed frame of Sledge running full speed at Annakus, taken by surprise Annakus turned, reached into her pocket and threw what looked like a small pebble at Sledges feet ,there was a flash and an explosion, the chamber rumbled ad Annakus stepped out into the sunlight just as large chunks of sand-stone fell, blocking the doorway and pushing a cloud of dust back into the room, it went dark, Tumbler felt around the floor trying to find Sledge and under the faint glow of the Wonder Piece he found Sledge, on his back coughing and gasping for air, "Get the Piece" he said wheezing so Tumbler ran over to the Piece in the wall, he couldn't reach, his fingertips were 2 inches below the bottom of the piece, he stood on tip toes, no good he still wasn't tall enough, he looked at his watch, 3:59pm, "I can't get it, I need your..!" but before he could finish his sentence it happened, the Piece vibrated and the room was filled with an almighty flash of green light, he put his hands over his eyes and saw stars bouncing around the room, Sledge rolled onto his front and covered his head with his arms and then they heard it, screaming, crashing, yells of terror coming from outside the temple.

"We need to get out of here now!" Panic engulfed Tumbler "The doorway has opened; we need to get out!"

Sledge got to his feet and stumbled to the doorway, he started lifting large pieces of sandstone to one side, eventually he made a gap big enough for them both to squeeze through.

Outside it was pitch black but how could this be, the sun was not due to go down for at least another hour, in amongst the chaos Tumbler saw the shape of something long, exceptionally long, moving its way through the crowd of tourists "Oh my god its Apep!"

"Who or What is Apep" Sledge cried "Apep or Apophis is The Great serpent, enemy of the sun god Ra, she was known in Ancient Egypt to come out daily to try and catch the sun from Ra and destroy it, she is why it's so dark, people can't see anything, if we don't do something now, she could actually put the Earth into complete darkness, we don't have long".

What they could see in the darkness Apep was at least 40ft, she was mostly black with a red/orange stripe running the full length of its body and its head was that of a Cobra with massive fangs hanging down from the top of its mouth like stalactites on the ceiling of a cave, its tail split into three and each one was thrashing around as it slipped across the sand.

They stepped into the darkness, shadows drifted past them like black ghosts, people were using their phone torches to see where they were heading, it looked like hundreds of shooting stars all passing by at once, like the night sky hand fallen to earth and was making the ground its own.

The long dark figure zigzagged in and out of the terrified crowd sometimes stopping for a minute and then thrusting forward as if it were a predator attacking it prey, now and again you would hear a scream of pain as people were knocked over in the panic, "How do we stop this?" ask Sledge in a strange, high-pitched voice.

Tumbler accessed the surrounding or what he could see anyway, he focuses on Apep and noticed if she got near someone with their phone light shining directly at it, she would dart the other way then it came to him, "light!" he said with a yelp, "Yeah that would be handy" Sledge replied sarcastically, "No I mean artificial light" replied Tumbler, Sledge was still a little unsure what he was going on about, "You going to have to explain" he said.

Tumbler turned to him and spoke so fast it was almost inaudible "Apep can block out natural light obviously that is why we can't see the sun however she is avoiding people with their phone torches on as she cannot stop it", then it sank in, Sledge looked at Tumbler in amazement "So if we can get enough artificial light on her in one go we could almost back her into a corner, is that what you are saying?" "Yes," replied Tumbler "and I know how," he reached into his other pocket and pulled out another marble sized pebble "With this" he stretched his arm out in the direction of Sledge and opened his palm "How is that going to work? You throw one of those and yes it will explode and produce some light but it won't last long enough" Sledge was confused for a moment "These are not the same" replied Tumbler "These are flash stones, you throw one of these behind you, it pops and produces a flash of light that lasts for 2 minutes, enough time to get away from a threat, something else The Protectors of the Septem are issued with if they come across danger, we would normally use them along with the Iter Stone in cases of emergency but this seems a better time than any, it's are only hope"

"So, what shall I do" enquired Sledge "What else do you have it that bag of yours" asked Tumbler, Sledge put his bag down and pulled out a grappling hook and a length of rope "Any good" he said with a smile, "Perfect" Tumblers brain was in overdrive now "As soon as I throw the stone you get the hook and rope around its head below its hood and take the other end and wrap it around its tail" "That easy! "remarked Sledge, the sarcasm in his voice growing every minute.

They waited for their opportunity and at the right moment Tumbler shouted "Now!" he ran in front of Apep, turned to face away from it and threw the Flash stone over his shoulder, there was an almighty glare that not only stopped Apep in its tracks but bought the remaining crowd to their knees, the space in front of Temple seemed like it was noon, as if the sun had been pointed directly at that one spot by an invisible force, Apep dropped its head to the ground as if it was trying to avoid the light "Go" Shouted Tumbler again and Sledge bounded towards Apep swinging the hook and rope around his head like a cowboy about to lasso a wild horse, he let go of the hook and it swung around Apeps head, it missed! He rolled it back around his arm, he started swinging again and let go, this time it hit the mark, Apep lunged forward dragging Sledge along the floor, Sledge managed to dig his heels into the ground, the rope slipping through his hands, Sledge let her gain a bit of distance and he then was parallel to the three whipping tails, he wrapped the rope around and around tight enough for it to pull Apeps head back towards her tail creating a "U" shape, she tried to straighten up but couldn't and with the remaining piece of rope Sledge tied it off o the first thing he could see, one of the six sandstone pillars at the front of the Temple.

People were still running around all over the place, smashing into each other, trampling the fallen and grabbing at loved ones arms to pull them away from the scene that was unravelling in front of their eyes then through the crowd Tumbler appears hand above his head and throws a marble straight into Apeps open mouth, he dropped to the ground, hands over his ears and "bang" bits of Apeps head including its fangs flew in every direction covering the onlookers and Sledge in blood and scales, Sledge heard a thud and one of the fangs landed in the ground to the left of him the other stuck into the sandstone rock above his head, Apeps tail continued to thrash for a good minute or so after its head had been removed then slowly it dropped to the ground and there was silence, the blackness that was covering the area began to fade and the remaining sunlight shone through, that's when the carnage became apparent, there were at least 30 bodies lying motionless, people were knelt down cradling heads of friends and loved one who had either been injured or passed on, others were in an embrace sobbing and there were 3 dead camels all lying next to each other still tethered to a deceased guide, it was Bes, Tumbler walked up to his motionless body, brushed his hand over Bes's eyes and closed his eyelids, he then draped one of the blankets from under the camels saddle over Bes and turned back to Sledge.

Sledge had that feeling he was being watched, he scanned the ridges above his head and that is when he saw her, Sledge tapped Tumbler on the shoulder and pointed in her direction, Annakus looked directly at the pair, patted the Satchel, and saluted like a solider saluting her superior and before they knew it, she vanished.

"Where has she gone now" Sledge asked not sure if he really wanted to know.

"The next location I guess" replied Tumbler "Which would be the Colosseum in Rome."

"Another plane!" Sledge hung his head "How long is this going to take this time, I'm knackered."

"Well, it's back to King Hussein International airport which if we leave now should take just under 3 hours and it's a 3 hour 30 minutes give or take a few minutes so we should land at Rome Ciampino Airport around 12:30am their time, plenty of time to rest up before." Tumbler interrupted Sledge "Before we face her again!"

"Unfortunately, yes, so we better make a move," they turned on their heels and set off for the airport, both wondering what they were about to face in Rome.

Chapter 8

Rome is beautiful, the architecture is breath-taking, and the history is amazing, all things that Sledge never thought he would get to experience even if it is under circumstances, he never imagined he would be involved in.

They landed in Rome Ciampino Airport around 1am, a little later than they originally thought but it was all good, still plenty of time before the 4pm deadline they had to try and stop from happening, 15hrs and counting, what could they do for 15hrs Sledge thought, "I know, Sleep" he turned to Tumbler who was in deep thought "Let's find somewhere to get our heads down for a bit, I need to sleep for a few hours in a bed not an airplane seat!" he cracked his neck which made the sound of someone walking over broken glass, Tumbler looked at him and grimaced "Yeah I get you, I could do with a few hours", they walked out of the airport and took a taxi to Rome city centre and checked into Hotel Artemide, it had large glass doors at the front of the building and looked very grand, Tumbler and Sledge looked out of place, with the only people visible at 2am where two men and one women dressed in business attire drunkenly stumbling through the main lobby looking like they had just finished entertaining a client as one of the men had his tie on his head and the women had her high heel shoes in her hand whilst the second male was holding her up, Tumbler and Sledge could just about hear one of the males say excitingly "I think we've got that one in the bag, promotion here I come" and punched the air in triumph.

Sledge and Tumbler checked into their rooms a bid each other what was left of a good night, they agreed to meet in the lobby at 8am sharp so they could set out their plan of action, Sledge dumped his bag on the floor, kicked off his shoes and fell back onto the bed, he was out as soon as his head hit the pillow.

Tumbler on the other hand lied on his bed staring at the ceiling thinking "What next?" and "What if?", he had different scenarios running through his head, "What would happen if Annakus succeeded?" was the biggest question he kept asking himself, he really did not want to think what the answer to that question could be, eventually after an hour he fell asleep and only woke when there was a knock at his door, "Who is it?" he shouted half hearted, still in between sleep and awake "It's me!" bellowed Sledge "Its 8:45am, I've been waiting in the lobby for 45 minutes!, What happened to 8am sharp?"

Tumbler looked at the clock on the wall, 8:46am, he jumped out of bed and answered the door, "Come in for a moment whilst I freshen up", Sledge bound into the room like a bull who had just been released in a bull fight, "So where do we go from here?" he asked Tumbler sitting in the chair in the corner of the room looking out of the window.

Tumblers room looked out over the cobbled street, tourists were starting to fill the street, maps in hand, shooting off in different directions on their own little adventures, one attraction being Trevi Fountain that was only a 12-minute walk from the Hotel.

Sledge continued to talk whilst Tumbler got ready in the bathroom "I went for a little walk whilst I was waiting for you and I saw a restaurant on the corner, thought we would grab a coffee, and something called a Sausage and Egg McMuffin before we head out" Tumbler poked his head around the door of the bathroom and said "Was this restaurant called McDonalds' by any chance?" he was trying not to laugh but then realised that Sledge hadn't stepped foot out of Killington in his life and there was no McDonalds' there so this was another new experience for him, plus the seriousness on Sledges face Tumbler thought "Best to not say anymore", he held back the smile and said "Yeah sounds good we will give it a go, are you sure you don't want to find something fried?" basing his comment on the food Sledge had eaten at the last 2 locations, Sledge looked at him and said, "It's got M.C and the beginning of the food title and the name is McDonalds, surely it's got to be something Scottish!" Tumbler just back into the bathroom, laughed a silent laugh and popped back out "Yeah we will go straight there."

They checked out of the hotel around 9:30am and strolled down the road to the McDonalds, Sledge had his first Sausage and egg McMuffin and thought it was OK, but it did not hit the spot but what "Food is Food."

"What's the plan of action then?" Sledge asked Tumbler wiping his mouth on his sleeve.

"Well" said Tumbler, "I think Annakus will wait until the last minute before she places the next wonder piece in its location in the Colosseum, so we have approximately 6 hours to waste, so aim to get there around 3pm, hopefully we will be able to stop her before she triggers the next doorway, I think we should make our way to the Trevi Fountain which is less than 15 minutes from here and only 1km from the Colosseum so about a 20 minute walk, see if we can spot Annakus early and wing it from there, lets chill around here and get to the Fountain for around 2:30ish, I'll buy you a Gelato at the Fountain" he winked.

"Wing it!" said Sledge surprised, "Yes" replied Tumbler "I've not had to deal with this before so even I am not sure what to expect, I was just told to look after the Pieces and given some basic knowledge around each 7 Wonder".

Sledge wiped his brow with his sleeve and started walking in the direction of the Trevi Fountain.

They arrived around 2:45pm at the Trevi Fountain and Sledges mouth dropped open in amazement, it was beautiful, its chalk-coloured Travertine stone glowed in the bright sunshine, its water glistened like a crystal, it was breath-taking and for a minute Sledge forgot what he was there for.

His sublime moment of peace was broken by Tumbler going into historian mode, "The Trevi Fountain is one of the oldest water sources in Rome" he said, "The fountain dates to ancient Roman times, since the construction of the Aqua Virgo Aqueduct in 19 B.C. that provided water to the Roman baths and the fountains of central Rome", "Amazing said Sledge taking another lick of his Pistachio Gelato.

Tourists were everywhere now, sitting on the edge of the fountain, selfie sticks and camera everywhere, people smiling, laughing, just generally enjoying themselves in the afternoon sunshine but then they felt something, at first it was a small shudder but the people that noticed including Tumbler and Sledge wrote it off as a lorry driving past, then the shudder became a violent shake, there was a deadly silence, then another shake and the ground below them cracked open, part of the wall surrounding the fountain broke open releasing gallons of water into the street, tourists were running for their lives, some were taken by surprise and rushed of their feet by the water, "What the hell is going on?" Sledge dropped his gelato on the floor and turned to Tumbler in shock "She got there early!" Tumbler said in panic, "she's worked out from the last 2 times that we were there first and this time she is using the Pieces power to delay us!"

"What?" screamed Sledge.

"She has put the Piece back already, she knows it won't trigger the doorway until 4pm but she is creating as much chaos as she can now to ensure it opens" Tumbler was in panic mode now, "We have to go!", he turned on his heel and Sledge had never seen him run so fast.

They rushed past cars that had spun out of control avoiding pedestrians frantically running across the roads, there was rubble strewn around the streets were parts of buildings had tumbled from the tremors, there was a man trapped inside a car that had flipped avoiding the rubble "We have to help!" shouted Sledge, "We can't" said Tumbler reluctantly "We need to get to the Colosseum and when we do we need to work out where the Piece is!"

"What do you mean work it out? I thought you would know straight away!" Sledge scratched his head.

"No" replied Tumbler "My father told me the locations of the Pieces, but the Colosseum could hold 50,000 people and it covers six acres, it's not going to be that easy to find and remember it won't be glowing green until 4pm when the 24hrs is up, let me think for a minute".

Chapter 9

They barged through the panicked crowd and reached the Colosseum entrance, Tumbler put his hand to his mouth and looked up at the sky as if he was trying to recall something, "I remember my father telling me an equation that would help me work out where the Piece would be placed but I can't quite remember how it goes", "Well get thinking" said Tumbler "Times ticking" pointing at an imaginary watch on his wrist, just then a tourist pushed past dropping a Tourist guide of the Colosseum, Tumbler picked it up and flicked through the pages "That's it" he read it out loud to an impatient Sledge ".The Colosseum could seat 50,000 people. It covers around six acres of land and is 620 feet long, 512 feet wide, and 158 feet tall. It took more than 1.1 million tons of concrete, stone, and bricks to complete the Colosseum."

"And?" said Sledge pointing at the invisible watch again.

"Well, 620 feet long+512 feet wide +158 feet tall = 1290, 50000 people capacity that's what the _L is, _L is roman numeral for 50,000, 50,000 divided by 1290 equals 38.75 feet from entrance and it covers 6 acres" Tumbler smiled.

"I'm lost" Sledge's face was covered in confusion, Tumbler sighed "Basically rounding it up we need to go thirty-six feet from the entrance and six rows up, the row we need will be marked with VI, roman numeral for six and at the beginning of that row will be the Piece, Simple" Tumbler smiled again.

"Left or right?" said Sledge pointing in both directions, "You go left and I'll go right" shouted Tumbler, the time was now 3:45pm, just as Sledge turned left a large boulder crashed in front of him pinning his bag to the ground, his arm was caught in the strap and he couldn't move, he tried shouting to Tumbler but the noise of the rumbles muffled out his calls, Tumbler was counting his steps, 35, 36, 37, 38 he turned and went up to the row with the VI, "Wrong way, The Piece isn't here!" he thought to himself, he looked in the direction of Sledge, "It's not.." but before he could finish his sentence, that's when he saw him trapped, struggling to free his right arm.

Tumbler ran as fast as he could to Sledges aid and out of the corner of his eye, he saw Annakus, he couldn't hear her, but he could see she was laughing, it was a maniacal laugh, the laugh of a mad person who was enjoying what she was witnessing, what she had created, "Reach into my bag" ordered Sledge "There should be a Bowie knife in a black sheath, cut the strap, hurry! We don't have much time", Tumbler found the knife and it sliced through the leather strap on the bag in one go, Sledge jumped to his feet and quickly counted out 38 paces and in his head he was saying "V, I, V,I" over and over "6 is VI, 6 rows up", he got to row 4 and he could see a faint green glow, row 5 was getting brighter and just before he could reach row 6 the Piece bust into a blinding green light that knocked him off his feet, he fell back 2 rows, he was too late, the ground at the centre of the Colosseum opened up, a hole the size of a small car appeared, it was the doorway, he turned and saw Annakus rubbing her hands together, still laughing and what he saw next made him lose his footings, it was a Lion but not a normal lion like you see in pictures in history books fighting the Gladiators, it was big, about the size of small elephant, it cleared Sledges 6ft 11 frame by at least another 4ft and it had almost black hair and a bright orange mane that made it look like its head was surrounded by flames, all this was relatively similar to what you know a lion to look like apart from one thing, it had a tail of a lizard, scaley and pointed at the tip, Sledge looked in the direction of Tumbler who had left his last position and had made his way towards Annakus.

"It's up to me again!" thought Sledge as he stood up, trying to make himself look taller than he already was, the creature lowered its head and roared an almighty roar that once again nearly knocked Sledge off his feet but he managed to hold firm, it bolted straight at him, Sledge dived to his right and the Lion hit the wall behind him and crashed to the floor, Sledge grabbed its tail and pulled it as hard as he could but what happened next took him by surprise, the whole tail came off in his hands, the Lion turned, Sledge stood in amazement with the tip of the tail in his hands and the end that was attached to the Lion on the floor 6ft in front of him, the Lion halted for a moment and Sledge could see the beginnings of a new tail growing back, he dropped the old tail, turned and ran towards the entrance of the Colosseum, he dropped and rolled just as the creature leaped at him and it cleared him by a good 5 feet and landed blocking the entrance, it roared again, Sledge rolled to his left just as the lion passed him and grabbed hold of a large chunk of its mane and swung onto its back, he was now hurtling across the Colosseum like a bull rider in a rodeo when suddenly the Lions front legs slipped out from underneath it, Sledge could see the handle of a Spatha, a long, straight sword used in Gladiator fights and the other end was plunged deep into the chest of the Lion, the thing that surprised Sledge the most was that attached to the handle end of the Spatha was Tumbler who was kneeling down, one leg stretched out behind him to balance himself and the other knee dug deep into the ground for leverage, his eyes were closed and his face was scrunched up like a prune, after what seemed like an eternity the Lion fell onto its side pinning Sledges leg underneath it and it laid there, its shallow breathing causing its ribs to move only slightly and small amounts of blood bubbling from its wound, Sledge managed to pull himself free and stood looking at the fallen creature, Suddenly out of nowhere it roared, its mouth wide open and something ran out, it was another Lion, about the size of a large dog, it looked like a smaller version of what they had just slayed, it turned and bolted towards the Doorway in the ground and disappeared into the light.

"What the hell just happened?" said a surprised Sledge "It's a Regenerator", said Tumbler "If killed it can produce a mirror image of itself but not with its original strength, it has to grow to build the power a fully grown Regenerator has which is why it went back into the Doorway, that's also why this one was able to grow back its tail when you pulled it off, it is a defensive mechanism that some lizards especially a salamander, if you cut off its tail in a few weeks, a near-perfect replacement grows, obviously this one is much stronger which is why it grew back within minutes and this gene also allows it to produce a mirror image of itself within minutes of its death, fascinating hey?"

"Yeah" said Sledge sarcastically "Thanks for the Natural history lesson, Mr Attenborough, anyway, did you get close enough to Annakus?"

"Sort of" replied Tumbler, "I got close enough to hear one word before she did her disappearing act again."

"And that word was?" questioned Sledge.

"Chichen" said Tumbler, "Chicken" said Sledge confused, "No Chichen" replied Tumbler "it's the fourth oldest new 7 Wonders, Chichen Itza in Yucatán, Mexico, that's where the next Doorway is, that's where she is headed now".

"Mexico!" cried Sledge, "How longs that going to take?"

"Roughly 19hrs, they are 7 hours behind us so we should arrive at Merida Airport around Midday if we leave now for Rome Ciampino Airport that gives us about 4hrs to reach the next Piece location".

"If we are going to be on another plane for 19hrs I need an aisle seat!" said Sledge yawning.

"No problem lets go" giggled Tumbler and of they went, destined for Mexico.

Chapter 10

Midday in Mexico is hot, the temperature on the airport clock showed 36.6°C, there was a mild breeze, but it was a warm one, hotter than Egypt, Sledge was sweating profusely, the hankie in his hand was dripping already and his beard and hair looked like he had just got out of a shower, there was no time to stop for food at this airport they had to get out and get to Chichen Itza quick and it was at least an hour and 40 minutes by bus, they just had to hope there was one outside ready to go, they made their way through the crowd of people all rushing in opposite direction either later for their flight or meeting family and friends picking them up from the airport, Tumblers head was down, focused on the job in hand, the noise of people talking drowned out all the other noises in the airport but for a moment Tumbler thought he heard someone near him say "Yahmi", he was sure he had heard the word before but didn't know why it stood out so much but just shook it off but then he heard it again but this time it was in the distance, he stopped in his tracks and was nearly bowled over by Sledge who was more focused on the buses parked outside than he was of what was in front of him, he managed to stop just centimetres away from Tumbler, What are you doing" he exclaimed, "I am sure someone said Yahmi" replied Tumbler and then he saw a flash of colour in the distance, a figure in purple and green flashed around the corner near the escalator and disappeared, he couldn't see its face as it was covered by the hood of the kaftan.

"We are definitely being followed" Tumbler was not sure if it were friend or foe, but he could not get that word out of his head, Lucky for them there was a large bus parked right outside the entrance of the airport and a man stood next to it with a clipboard in his hand ticking off people as they go on.

The clipboard guy greeted Sledge and Tumbler with a chirpy "Buenos Dias, names please," "We aren't on the list" stated Tumbler "We really need a ride to Chichen Itza, but we are on deadline, do you have any seats free, please say you do" he begged.

The man flicked through the paperwork on his clipboard and ran down the pages with his chewed biro, he looked up at the pair and firmly replied "I am fully booked however I am waiting on 2 more people; they are late as I should have left 5 minutes ago but if they don't show in the next 5 minutes you can have their seats, but I will have to charge you double", "Not a problem" replied Tumbler in a grateful voice, his fingers crossed on both hands, he looked at the guy's name badge below the emblem Oriente, the bus company he worked for, "Thank you so much Ricardo", Ricardo grinned and broke open a new carton of cigarettes, "smoke?" he offered Tumbler a cigarette, "No thanks" Tumbler waved his hand politely and looked at his watch, the 5 minutes was up and Ricardo dropped his cigarette on the floor and put it out with his shoe, "Jump on and let's get going" he took Tumbler and Sledges money "Seats 1 and 2 row 1 , right at the front on the left" Sledge put his bag into the overhead storage and sat on the outside seat so he could stretch his legs.

Ricardo grabbed the handset to the left of his steering and his loud, Mexican voice filled the bus "Ok, hope you are all ready for your adventure in Mexico, next stop Chichen Itza, this will be a non-stop drive so if anyone needs the toilet you will have to hold it as it is broken, sorry about that, it will take us approximately 1 hour and 39 minutes and the temperature outside is a lovely 36°c but you will be happy to know that the air con is not broken so I will get that going when we set off, please put on your seat belts and get ready for a real bus ride" he grinned and turned on the engine, the bus burst into life and they were off, he had only just turned the bus around when in his drivers mirror he could see a couple waving their arms frantically in the air, Ricardo opened his window, waved out of the window and mouthed "Your 10 minutes late, sorry!", closed his window back up and drove off down the road, Tumbler and Sledge slid down in their seats and pretended they couldn't see the women of the couple waving her hands in the air and pointing at her partner, she was tapping her finger on her watch and that's as much as they could make out, "Hate to be him" smirked Sledge and closed his eyes.

Half an hour into the journey Sledge was awoken by Tumblers voice, he was having a general chitchat with Ricardo when he heard Ricardo say, "So you guys are in a hurry then, what are you doing in Mexico apart from visiting Chichen Itza, you're not exactly dressed like normal tourists are you?" pointing at the large leather boots and thick trousers Sledge was wearing, "Mind you, there was a women waiting outside the airport this morning and I thought she stood out as she was wearing a long black dress and carrying a leather satchel, I remember thinking that she is going to feel the heat in that dress when the sun starts breaking through!".

Tumbler and Sledge looked at each other and simultaneously yelled "Annakus."

"Come to think about it" Ricardo remarked "She approached me and asked if I had seen two guys that matched your description, are you meant to be meeting her, is that why you're in a rush, not late are you?."5.

"I hope not" stuttered Tumbler looking at Sledge confused, "Why was she waiting at the airport, surely she would have just gone straight to Chichen Itza, I don't understand what she could achieve by waiting at the airport for us!"

"Maybe she has had a change of heart, maybe she wants to give up the bag and call it a day" remarked Sledge.

"I very much doubt it!" replied Tumbler, "She has been searching for the Pieces for years, she isn't just going to hand them back just like that."

"Out of interest what was she wearing Ricardo? Asked Tumbler inquisitively.

"Odd question" replied Ricardo "she was wearing a long black dress; she must have been damn hot."

"Why does it matter?" said Sledge "come to think of it I can answer that myself, you know she was wearing a black dress, we saw he on top of the mountain back in Petra."

"It doesn't matter, how much longer do we have before we get there Ricardo?"

Ricardo looked back at Tumbler and grinned "Your just as bad as my kids, we will get there when we get there" he laughed "No seriously we have just over an hour left, it will be fine, you will get there to meet your friend."

"Friend, she's no friend" Sledge just shrugged that remark off and went back to napping but Tumbler still couldn't get the image of the purple and green kaftan disappearing behind that kiosk back in Wadi Musa out of his mind or seeing it in the airport, he was also thinking why the word yahmi was so familiar, his eyes were getting heavy now and not much time had passed before he drifted off next to an already snoring Sledge.

Chapter 11

They pulled up at Chichen Itza at around 2pm and the hustle and bustle of tourists was mind boggling, at least 90% of them carrying rucksacks and looking in their late teens to early twenties, on a gap year spending their time back packing.

The ruined ancient Maya city of Chichen Itza occupies an area of 4 square miles so it was not going to be an easy task locating Annakus amongst the bustling crowd and there were no hills, it was flat like a football field, so Tumbler and Sledge agreed to split up and meet in an hour by the main temple El Castillo or Temple of Kukulcán as its also known as.

"Which one is that?" enquired Sledge.

"It's the one right in the middle, it is a Mesoamerican step-pyramid that dominates the centre of the Chichen Itza, that one there" Tumbler pointed at the large, grey pyramid looking structure with the large steps running up all four sides to the flat top.

They split up and went their separate ways and it was not too long before Tumbler felt a tap on the shoulder, as he was turning around, he said "That was quick, have." but before he could finish his heart sank, looking down at him with that gaunt face and long black hair was Annakus.

"Hello Tumbler, so that's what you look like up close, you have your fathers' eyes" declared Annakus, "Have you been enjoying your trips?"

He was not sure how to respond, Tumbler felt his body shaking but not in fear, with anger "What the hell are you doing, why are you so obsessed with causing all this destruction, your killing innocent people for what, for fun?" his hands wanted to grab her throat, but he held back.

"I'm not doing it for fun, although it is pretty exciting every time I put a Piece back, gives me a little tingle" she gave a little shudder of excitement "No its to get back at him, for all the things I did for him, all the places I followed him around listening to those stories, just wanting to know the truth and he just kept telling me he had made them up to entertain the children" she made little gestures with her fingers to suggest it was exaggerated "Your Great grandfather thought I was stupid, just another silly women to him who was to do what she was told, I knew they were true and he left me when I found the Pieces in his office, he took Joshinda, your father and the Wonder Pieces and left me, he left me with no one after all those years" her voice was getting sharper, more angry by the minute.

"But why do you feel the right to have them now?" Tumbler looked down to where the Satchel should be, but it was not there, "Where are they" he inquired.

"They are safe" she assured him "and I have the right to hold them, it's my birth right as the daughter of the Protector of the Septem."

"But it's not your birth right" snarled Tumbler "You know the tradition, it is passed on to the male in the family, my Great Grandfather, your father did not have a son so the next in line was my father, your nephew!"

"It's a stupid tradition" Annakus snarled "I knew everything about those Pieces, I should do I listened to the stories enough, it should have been me Protecting those Pieces, I could have trained your father but your Great grandfather wouldn't move from tradition and then he took my boy away from me and left me alone, that's when I told myself that I wasn't going to be used, I was going to find those Pieces and use them for the purpose they were created for, to cleanse the earth".

"Hang on a minute!" Tumbler said with confusion in his voice "What do you mean "My Boy," you never had children" he assumed she had made a mistake.

"My boy, Luka" she said with what sounded like sadness in her voice.

"That was my father's name, but wait, his mother was Joshinda, he told me stories of when he was growing up and how much she loved him, what she taught him, why would you say, "My boy," Tumbler was trying to get his head around what was being said.

"He was my son, your Great grandfather thought I was a threat when I found the Pieces and took him away from me when he was a baby, Joshinda raised him as her own, your father only found out the truth just before you were born, I tracked him down after years of searching, your Great

Grandfather and Joshinda both died during the Mexican-American War, the same year the 1849 Treaty of Guadalupe Hidalgo ended the War which was unfortunate for them" she said sarcastically, "Your father was 169 years old, I had the chance to take the satchel then but seeing him for the first time in all those years broke my heart, I gave him the photo then he used the Iter stone and I never saw him again, why else would your father be carrying a photo of me, bit weird carrying a photo of your crazy Auntie don't you think, would you not think it would be a photo of Joshinda if she really was his mother" Annakus paused waiting for a response from Tumbler but it never came, "I heard your father made his fortune during the same year, Californian gold rush, where else would you have got all that money you are using now!"

Just as Tumbler was about to react, he heard a voice behind him bellowing like a crazed buffalo.

"Tumbler" hollered Sledge "Get away from her now!" and as Tumbler turned his back on a charging Sledge she was gone, "What did she say" barked Sledge "What did she tell you?" "Did you get the bag?"

"One question at a time" begged Tumbler "No I didn't get the bag, she didn't have it on her, and I don't think you are going to believe what she told me, I didn't at first."

"What!" pleaded Sledge just wanting answers "She told me she is my grandmother, and she took the Pieces to conduct a 341-year-old vendetta against my Great Grandfather, she believes he stole her birth right as Protector of the Septem".

"But she couldn't, its tradition for the male or so you told me" Said Sledge "And anyway Joshinda was your grandmother!"

"Obviously not" remarked Tumbler "but it does not really matter, we still have to stop her!"

They scoured the crowd looking for where Annakus could have gone, she was nowhere to be seen.

Shortly after her confrontation with Tumbler Annakus returned to the hotel she had been hiding out in and suddenly a short, olive skinned man rushed past her and out of the double doors leading to the road, as she walked up the corridor she noticed the door to her room was ajar, she silently pushed the door open and the room was a mess, bed sheets were on the floor, drawers had been pulled out and then she saw it, the wardrobe doors were open and her heart sank, she rushed to the wardrobe and waved her hands over what was now a vacant space, the bag was gone, she rushed to the window and saw the olive skinned man dart around a corner, she leapt out of the window and onto the fire escape and made her way down the ladder, it rattled as she rushed down it, dropping the last few rungs to the street below, she hitched up her long dark dress and flew around the corner and up the street where she had last seen the olive skinned man, she saw him elbow his way through the crowd and into a small shop selling Mexican souvenirs, Annakus followed him as he exited through the rear of the shop and into another street, she stopped for a moment and noticed a small alleyway, she turned and moved slowly up the alley and just as she was about to exit onto the street the olive skinned man rushed past her, stopping in his tracks as she stepped out in front of him and with one swift movement of her foot she bought him tumbling to the ground, the remaining Pieces falling out of the bag which was still under his arm and scattering over the street.

"Who put you up to this" she snarled at the olive-skinned man, he looked up at her a just one word came out of his mouth, "Yahmi," she placed her foot over the fingers on his left hand and pressed down, "I will ask you again, who put you up to this? She pushed down harder on his fingers hearing a crunch, the olive-skinned man winched "I do not know" he said in broken English "I do not get name, they paid me to find lady in black, told me to find bag and leave it."

"Leave it where" Annakus said through gritted teeth, the olive-skinned man looked at her in pain "In rubbish bin by café."

Annakus picked up the bag, put the Pieces inside and slung it over her bony shoulder "well he is going to be extremely disappointed" she cackled "what did this person look like."

"I do not know, was wearing green mask" his voice now trembling with fear as Annakus pushed down harder on his already broken fingers.

"A green mask!" she looked at him blankly, "well you tell this green masked person when you see them that they need to come up with something better than a simple-minded street thief before they can get their hands on this bag", she turned her heel on the olive-skinned man's fingers and kick him away, he stood up holding his fingers and ran back off down the alley.

An hour had past, and Tumbler and Sledge were now making their way to the doorway at the base of the temple when they felt something, the familiar rumble, the hint of green shimmering from the top of El Castillo and that is when they spotted the shadow figure of Annakus, Piece in hand.

"What is the time?" screamed Tumbler, Sledge looked at his watch "Its 3:59 and just as he finished saying fifty-nine there was the burst of green and the doorway at the base of the Temple opened but this time there was no beast, no large serpent or creature, nothing!

"What's going on, why has nothing happened" but just as Sledge had finished his sentence, he felt something tug on his bag, when he looked down there was nothing there, but his bag suddenly felt lighter, two daggers lighter, he panicked "There gone!" he shouted.

"What's gone? Tumbler exclaimed.

"My two knives, the Dirk and the Bowie!" Sledge yelled "I felt something tug on my bag and when I looked down there was nothing there, but the bag was open, and they were missing."

Just as Tumbler was about to suggest pick pocketing, he felt something brush past him, it felt like a child but when he looked around there were no children to be seen, then he felt it again but this time it was a tug on his pocket, he then heard the guy stood next to him shout "My phone has gone!"

and then another voice "My camera!" and more and more voices announcing that personal items were missing, Tumbler had no idea what was going on and then he spotted one, "An Alux!" he cried.

"What on earth is an Alux" Sledge asked.

"Some Mayan people believe that the Alux are called into being when a farmer builds a little house on his property, most often in a maize field. For seven years, the Alux will help the corn grow, summon rain, and patrol the fields at night, whistling to scare off predators or crop thieves. At the end of seven years, the farmer must close the windows and doors of the little house, sealing the Alux inside. If this does not happen, the Alux will run wild and start playing tricks on people, these must be the ones that were not locked up" Tumbler sighed.

"Are they dangerous?" asked Sledge, then he saw one for himself, it was knee height and looked like a squat, tubby looking thing with pointy ears and its hair up in a bun, "They look like children?"

"They aren't dangerous but are bad enough to cause enough of a distraction to allow Annakus to flee, she knows that all they will do is cause mischief however, they could cause enough damage to cause bigger problem" Tumbler declared.

"Like pinching peoples belongings, eventually someone is going to blame the person stood next to them" suggested Sledge, then it happened, in the distance they heard a loud voice shout "Have you taken my girlfriend's purse?" then another voice replied "Why would I take her purse, I think your girlfriend has taken my phone!" and then Sledge and Tumbler saw the two guys rolling on the floor throwing punches at each other whilst their partners screamed at each other and onlookers tried to break them up, then the whole place erupted, fights everywhere and every now and again you could hear whistling, a distinct sound of an Alux as it tries to scare away what it sees as a predator.

"So, what do we do?" asked Sledge looking down at Tumbler but for a minute Tumbler looked a little distracted, he was looking at the shadow on Annakus at the top of the temple and all of a sudden he saw a smaller figure sneaking up behind her, it was an Alux, it reached out and grabbed the satchel from beside Annakus and ran full speed down the steps, "it's got the Satchel" said Tumbler, "Its stolen the bag from Annakus!" he was both gobsmacked at what he had just seen, pleased she didn't have it but in panic as he didn't know where it was going with it, so many emotions ran through Tumbler all in one go.

"We need to catch the little bastard before he opens the bag and finds the other Pieces" stuttered Sledge in a fit of panic, he barged through the crowd and lunged for the Alux but it was too small and dipped out of his way shooting up the other staircase on the opposite side of the temple, Sledge tried to intercept it by running along one of the ledges of the temple but it was too quick and then he saw Annakus on the other side, she reached out and grabbed the Alux by its hair, pulled the Satchel out of its hands and threw the Alux off the edge, it flew through the air and hit the ground below, for a moment it writhed around and then it disintegrated into a heap of dust, "I couldn't get to it in time!" he shouted down to Tumbler "Annakus got it back before I could stop it" Sledge was annoyed with himself as the satchel was just out of his grasp, he could have stopped it all and now he was kicking himself that he couldn't get it, he felt like he had let Tumbler down.

"There was nothing you could have done about it" Tumbler reassured Sledge "It just wasn't meant to be, we will get it eventually."

They climbed to the top of the temple so they could get a better view, it was carnage down there, people were fighting everywhere, and they kept seeing little flashes of blue as the Alux zipped in and out of the people, amongst the crowd they saw Annakus, bag on her shoulder making, her way to the edge of the chaos, she turned for a minute and saw Sledge and Tumbler at the top of El Castillo, she waved at them sarcastically and blew a little kiss in Tumblers direction, Tumbler shuddered at the thought of a kiss from her connecting with his check and took a little shift to one side as if to avoid the kiss landing, then there was that all familiar popping sound and Annakus was gone.

"Where's granny gone?" joked Sledge, he looked at Tumbler, he wasn't impressed by the comment, so Sledge quickly moved on "So, where has she popped off to now?" and just as Tumbler was about to reply they saw a swarm of police move in from the left and start dispatching the unruly crowd, some were put into handcuff and lead off with partners not far behind shouting "It was defence" or "The little blue guy took it, not him, he didn't do anything" and they could see the police just shaking their heads in disbelief and laughing at their colleagues, then Sledge caught a glimpse of an Alux standing just on the edge of the entrance to the doorway where he had first appeared, it was waving frantically and then another appeared from behind a large guy with a back pack, it took the guys water bottle that was hanging on the side of the bag, tipped it upside and the contents fell out all over the little Alux, it threw the bottle to the ground, jumped on it a few times and ran over to its friend that was waiting by the entrance, the second one jump through the doorway and the one that was waving followed it in and that was that, they were gone, but for how long?, this was no longer Tumbler and Sledges problem, their problem had disappeared like she always does and they now needed to find where.

"To answer your earlier question "said Tumbler, "Chichen Itza was number as number 4 so if she is familiar with the locations as she should be by now then she has gone to Peru".

"Peru! who is she looking for now, Paddington! is she going to steal his marmalade sandwiches" Sledge yelled trying to shed a little humour on the situation.

"Whose Paddington" Tumbler said puzzled.

"Don't worry" replied Sledge, realising that the joke had gone straight over Tumbler's head.

Tumbler continued "Yes Peru, the 5th location is Machu Picchu" he hesitated for a minute as he knew Sledge wasn't going to like the next bit, so he said it as quick as he could hoping Sledge wouldn't take it in, "It's a 14-and-a-half-hour journey!", Sledges mouth moved but no words came out but his eyes said it all, "Well it's not that long on the plane its only just under 10hrs but we then need to fly from Jorge Chávez International Airport to Cusco which is about an hour and a half then the easiest way to get from Cusco to Machu Picchu is to take the train to Aguas Calientes. It's a scenic 3.5-hour trip along tracks that run right along the Urubamba River in the Sacred Valley, with dramatic canyon walls on either side, its apparently very beautiful" Tumbler tried his best to big it up so Sledge had something to look forward to but it didn't seem to be working, "The time now is 6:25pm so let's get the bus back to the airport as there is a flight at 9pm, Peru is an hour ahead so that should get us there for around 7am their time, plenty of time to get to Machu Picchu for about midday, 4hrs before the 4pm deadline but who knows what Annakus has planned this time for our arrival?"

"Come on then" Sledge huffed "sooner we leave the sooner we get there I suppose and I'm starving so wouldn't mind grabbing something to eat at the airport before our flight."

"I'm with you on that one" Tumbler smiled and rubbed his little round belly and off they went ready to embark on their next adventure both wondering what was in store.

Chapter 12

The flight to Peru was the worst so far, Sledge had not slept at all due to the turbulence and the arm rest had indentations from where his fingers had been squeezing for hours, his eyes had dark shadows under them and they looked like they had sunk deep into his skull, Tumbler on the other hand was sleeping like a baby and was used to these types of journeys, he looked fresh as a daisy which did not, please Sledge.

Sledge gave Tumbler a little nudge to wake him up but made it out as if his arm had slipped, "You awake?"

Tumbler shot bolt upright, knocking the seat in front of him and getting a nasty look from the guy in front whose seat was in the reclining position just inches from Tumblers knees, "I am now!" he said with a yawn "What's the matter?"

"I was just thinking about what Annakus said to you at Chichen Itza, 341 years stewing on a grudge must make someone a tad annoyed for being abandoned but trying to wipe out entire populations is a bit extreme; don't you think?" Sledge slouched in his seat and waited for a response, but Tumbler had his eyes closed again, Sledge gave him another subtle nudge, "Did you hear any of that?"

Tumbler sat bolt upright once again and not quite awake, "What?, Yeah I did, sorry!" he then began to think about what Sledge was saying, "I remember my father saying that something didn't feel right for a while before my Great grandfather abandoned her, she was always a bit sketchy and on edge, when I think about it now it wasn't long after she had found the passage under his desk leading to the Wonders room, I think she had worked it out a long time before and was waiting for the right moment and when my Great grandfather caught her and took the pieces away along with my father and Joshinda she just had a meltdown and went mad!".

"Makes sense" remarked Sledge still slumped in his seat but now sipping on a small bottle of Jack Daniels the air flight attendant had bought around whilst Tumbler was sleeping.

Before they could say anymore the pilot came over the tannoid, "We will be beginning our descent into Jorge Chávez International Airport, the time is 6:34am and the temperature on the ground is twenty Celsius, a lovely morning in Peru so clip in your seatbelts and enjoy the last 20 minutes before we touch down in Callao.

"20 Celsius, I can deal with that" sighed Sledge.

They touched down and Sledge looked out of his window, the sun was just about up and the Sky had a breath-taking orange and yellow glow, there wasn't much around the airport apart from a few Hills but these looked like they were on fire against the Sky, for a minute Sledge felt tranquillity flood over him, he felt relaxed for the first time since leaving Killington but that was short lived when Tumbler woke up and grabbed his coat from the overhead "Come on!" he said sharply to Sledge, "We need to get through checkout and to the plane that is going to take us to Cusco, it takes off in just under 90 minutes!", he was trying to push past other passengers that were plodding their way down the walkway to the terminal when a tall guy in a suit grabbed his shoulder "Slow down buddy you're not going to get through check in any quicker by barging past people like that short stuff", suddenly the suited guy for a large, rough hand on his shoulder, he looked around to see a huge red haired, red bearded guy looking down at him "Enough with the short stuff pal, if you knew why he was rushing I'm sure you wouldn't have stopped him the way you did!" Sledge's eyes were piercing through the guy's skull, "Sorry bud" said the suited guy in a slightly whimpering voice "You carry on" Sledge smile to him then at Tumbler who had a little grin on his face and they both continued past the crowd to the check in gate for their short flight to Cusco.

They landed in Cusco just shortly after 9:45 AM, "Where do we go from here?" enquired Sledge.

"Well," said Tumbler thinking for a minute "Poroy is about 25 minutes by road from Cusco city so we will grab a taxi the journey time by train is 3 hours and 20 minutes and the train stop just once at Ollantaytambo station before ending at Aguas Calientes, once we get to Aguas Calientes we can take a short shuttle bus or hike up to Machu Picchu".

"I'm not hiking!" exclaimed Sledge, "Shuttle buses it is."

"I'm with you on that one" winked Tumbler "Plus we can get something to eat on the train and take in the scenery, should get us there with plenty of time so we should arrive around 1:30 PM they haled a taxi, jumped in the back seat and set off to catch the train in Poroy.

They stood on the platform and watched the cream and green train that was going to take them to Machu Picchu slowly grind to a stop, they climbed aboard and looked around what was going to be their transport for the next 3 hours, The car they were admiring had comfortable looking seats which pleased Sledge, folding tables and panoramic windows, there was Latin American music playing through the speakers and Sledges eyes were drawn to the on-board service advertising a selection of drinks made with Andean fruits and herbs, then he noticed it said "Non-alcoholic" at the end of the title so decided he would give that a miss, he ordered himself something of the menu called Cuy Chactado, he took it to his seat and demolished it in less than a few minutes, Tumbler let him finish and said pretending not to know what it was that Sledge had just eaten, "Was that nice?", Sledge looked at him funny "Yeah why?", "Oh no reason" giggled Tumbler.

Sledge was getting concerned now "It looked fried, so I went with it".

"Tumbler couldn't wipe the grin of his face, "you and your fried stuff", he couldn't contain his excitement anymore, "You have just eaten Fried Guinea pig", he burst out laughing and Sledge went a little green for a minute then just blew off the comment.

"Um, who would have thought, actually quite nice to be fair", then he went and ordered another, Tumbler just shook his head.

The train winded through the picturesque scenery, past green mountains and large flowing rivers, the sound of the tracks was quite soothing and Tumbler nodded off for a while when suddenly the train jolted to a holt, people were looking out of their windows trying to work out what had happened and at the front of the train Tumbler could see the driver stood beside the track looking at the floor, he got out shortly followed by Sledge and they both walked along the grass being careful not to lose their footing, as the noise of the gushing river echoed through the valley Sledge and Tumbler reached the driver and saw a landslide was blocking the tracks, then Tumbler saw that all familiar black figure standing high up in the hills, that laugh enhanced by the high mountains surrounding the train and then she was gone again.

Tumbler turned to Sledge and whispered, "This is Annakus, she is trying to delay us!".

Sledge looked at the pile of rocks and dirt and stroked his long red beard for a minute, then before Tumbler could say anything Sledge was pulling large rocks from the pile and rolling them down into the river below, "These rocks aren't going to move themselves are they!" and he pushed another the size of Tumblers off the edge causing a splash that made the train driver jump, the driver then climbed into the crew compartment and grabbed a shovel and started moving the mud that had built up under the wheelset as Sledge continued to move the rocks, an hour later the track was cleared and the train set off again.

"That's put us behind, but we should still arrive around 2:30pm, not ideal but we can live with it," said Tumbler.

"That is if Annakus doesn't appear again" replied Sledge angrily, washing the grime of his hands that were already cracked and grubby from years of blade smithing.

The trained pulled up at Aguas Calientes station around 2:34pm just a few minutes later than expected, they jumped off and headed for the small shuttle bus waiting to take the excited tourists to the Citadel located in the Machu Picchu District within Urubamba Province above the Sacred Valley on a 2,430-metre mountain ridge surrounded by lush green mountains, when they arrived Tumbler looked at Sledge and in a soft, gentle voice said "I've heard stories of this place but the stories don't give it justice, its breath-taking", he took in his surrounding and just for a moment he forgot why he was there until Sledge tapped in on the shoulder "Sorry bud, time to get back to the real world", tumbler looked up at Sledge with disappointment "I suppose" he sighed and starting walking towards the entrance.

They stood outside La Sun Gate, the main entrance into the Inca city, in the distance they could see Llamas grazing on the lush green grass, this was the first time Sledge had seen a llama and he was fascinated, such a beautiful animal, their brown and cream coats shining against the Peruvian sun.

Sledges moment of peace was broken by another one-off Tumblers facts that seemed to come with no warning, "Did you know?" Tumblers announced, "The llamas of Machu Picchu were so important to the Incan society that hunting them was forbidden, they were even used by the Inca priests in religious ceremonies."

"Fascinating" said Sledge with just enough sarcasm in his voice to make Tumbler believe he wasn't really interested, however he was, he had secretly began to like Tumblers facts, he had learned so much during his time with Tumbler that he felt like parts of his brain that had seemed empty for so long were beginning to fill up, "It will be useful one day" Sledge said to himself and then another Tumbler fact was thrown at him from nowhere.

"Did you know, the city was not discovered until 1911" Tumbler looked at Sledge waiting for a reaction, there was none, Sledge just grinned and walked through the sun gate into the city, the temperature was a satisfying 26°c and the breeze was just right, Sledge knew in his heart that this tranquillity wouldn't last long but made the most of it anyway, they had at least an hour before the inevitable would kick off, that if they couldn't stop it.

"We need to find the Intihuatana Stone" said Tumbler "It was designed as an astronomic clock by the Incas, it is a ritual stone and are arranged to point directly at the sun during the winter solstice, this is where the Piece more than likely originates from."

They asked a tour guide for direction, he pointed in the distance and then began giving a speech of the history of Machu Picchu, Sledge stopped him mid-sentence and pointed towards Tumbler, "He could tell you things about this place that you don't want to know" he winked, and the tour guide just looked at him weirdly, turned towards a group of hikers and began his speech again.

Chapter 13

They eventually arrived at the Intihuatana stone and it didn't take long for Tumbler to find the empty space where the Piece went, there were 2 circles carved into the stone and the Piece would go into the circle on the right, the space was empty which was a good sign but for how long, Tumbler looked at his watch, 3:32pm, they had less than 30 minutes to locate Annakus, they were in a good position ad could see the crowd wondering around the site, groups taking photos and couples with children climbing on the rocks, all trying to get that perfect family photo of their once in a lifetime experience, Tumbler kept seeing flashes of what he thought was Annakus but realised it was just shadows of the children running in and out of the many terraces that littered the city.

Suddenly they saw the tour guide they spoke to earlier waving in their direction, Tumbler and Sledge looked at each other, he was saying something but was just too far away for them to hear, Tumbler consulted his watch again, 3:41pm, they had time to get to the guide to find out what was so important, they made their way closer and as they approached the guide they noticed his eyes were black and vacant, "Hey buddy" Sledge clicked his fingers in the guides face, nothing, he did it again, then the tour guide opened his mouth and muttered 2 words that he kept repeating, Sledge leaned in, "To late" the guide whispered, Sledges face went pale, "What did he say?" asked Tumbler, Sledge looked back at the Intihuatana stone then back at Tumbler, he could see

Annakus standing over the stone with the Piece in her hand, "It's another distraction" gasped Tumbler, his heart sank as he heard that unmistakable cackle coming from Annakus, he could see the crazy enjoyment in her eyes as she plunged the Piece into the vacant gap in the stone, the pair rushed at Annakus, it was a good steep climb back up to the Intihuatana stone then half way there they stopped, the Piece glowed green but something wasn't right, 4:01pm and nothing happened, the Piece just stayed glowing, no bright burst of green light like the other times, no sudden explosion of thunder, rain, wind, no beasts, what was happening?, Sledge looked at Tumbler, Tumbler looked at Sledge "What the hell is going on?" asked Sledge, Tumbler was racking his brain trying to figure things out then suddenly Sledge shouts "It not in, something is stopping it making contact!" Sledge could see Annakus panicking, what had she done wrong then Tumbler noticed something in the bottom corner of the Piece, for a minute he was overcome with joy, "looks like someone has stuck their chewing gum in the space, I never thought I would say this but thank god for littering" but his glee was short lived, Annakus saw it too, she lunged for the gum and pulled it out with her long, blackened nails, it stretched a good foot before it pinged out of its resting spot, she threw it to the floor and forced the Piece back in and there it was, the explosion of green light, it blinded Sledge and Tumbler and knocked them both off their feet, the ground shook and part of the Intihuatana stone crumbled under the vibrations, large parts of the terraces below them broke away and showered down over the edge of the mountain knocking tourists off their feet and carrying them down the mountain face to their death, then they heard a scream, they turned and saw a female tourist being dragged into an open doorway, she screamed again, the blood curdling scream sent shivers down Tumblers spine and then she went silent, blood was running out of the door way, the sound of bones crunching echoed through the mountains, another group of tourists dashed past the doorway, one slipped on the blood soaking the ground but managed to keep his footing but the 2 following him where not as lucky, the first lost his footing and landed on his back and the second crashed into him, they both laid there dazed for a second and then out of the darkness a white, two wrinkled hands with long bony fingers and dark black nails reached out and grabbed bot guys feet, they scratched at the ground trying to get some form of grip but the hands were too strong, they were pulled into the darkness, their faces frozen with fear, one managed to grab the wall to the right of the doorway for a few brief seconds but lost his grip and was gone, more blood ran out of the doorway and mixed with the blood from the women before, bones snapped and there was silence.

For the first time Tumbler saw all the colour rush from Sledge's face, his month was wide open as if he were about to say something, but no sound came out, eventually Sledge looked at Tumbler "Who or what the hell is in that doorway?"

"It can't be!" replied Tumbler, "I've heard stories but always thought it was just myth."

"What are you thinking?" asked Sledge.

"I think its Pishtaco" began Tumbler "According to folklore, a Pishtaco is an evil monster like man often a stranger and often a white man, which would explain the white bony hands, who seeks out unsuspecting victims to kill them and abuse them in many ways. The legend dates back to the Spanish conquest of South America, Primarily, Pishtaco has been known to steal the victim's body fat for various cannibalistic purposes, Pishtaco derives from the local Quechua-language word "*pishtay*" which means to "behead, cut the throat, or cut into slices, that would explain all the blood".

"Well thanks for that detailed explanation!" Sledge wiped his brow, "How do we kill it?"

Tumbler thought for a moment, "Apparently they have 2 weaknesses, Silver, they are vulnerable to weapons made of silver or Severing Their Proboscis basically cutting off their sucking appendage with a silver blade will also kill a Pishtaco".

Sledge scratched his head, "Well I can see two issues there, one we don't have any silver and two we don't have any knives made of silver, so I hope you have another idea otherwise we might as well say goodbye to every remaining living person here."

"Hang on!" Tumbler reached into Sledge's bag, pulled out the Dirk, and waved it in his face, "Use this."
"Well, there is another issue" stated Sledge, "The blade is made of steel."
"But the handle isn't" grinned Tumbler, you're a bladesmith, surely you can turn the handle into a blade?"

"It's possible" said Sledge "I'll give it a go, but It won't stay sharp for long as Silver doesn't hold an edge well."

"We need to try" Said Tumbler "It's our only hope and we only have one shot so make it as sharp as you can and get close enough to Pishtaco to only need one cut."

"Hang on, what do you mean get close enough to only need one cut?" Sledge knew exactly what Tumbler meant but his brain was trying to distance itself from reality that it did not catch on for a moment.

"Your all muscle" winched Tumbler, "ninety% of my body is fat, Pishtaco will be drooling if it saw little fat me waddling over to it with a knife, at least you have strength and the ability to wrestle with it if you were to get into a tussle with it."

Sledge dropped his head and sighed, he grabbed the Dirk from Tumblers outstretched arm, took a large rock and flattened the edge of the silver handle as much as he could, he took a small Whetstone out of the side pocket of the bag and brushed it over the flat edge, brushing it over his hairy arm until it started to shave the hair clean off, eventually he turned to Tumbler "let's get this shit done" and marched off towards the bloody entrance of the doorway.

As they reached the doorway they cautiously poked their heads into the darkness and could just make out the bodies of the 3 tourists but it was unnervingly silent, they stepped into the darkness and suddenly a white, bony figure dashed past them, knocking the Dirk out of Sledges hand and throwing Tumbler to the ground, it exited the doorway and was gone, the pair collected themselves, picked up the Dirk off the floor and watched as Pishtaco leaped over a group of backpacker and grabbed one by the strap of the camera hanging around her neck and pulled her off the edge of one of the terraces, she screamed and went silent.

Sledge and Tumbler reached the edge of the terrace and saw the poor girls body lying in a heap on the ground, they looked up and saw more bodies scattered all over the other terraces, it was a massacre, "How could one thing cause all this carnage" Sledge could not believe his eyes.

"It's not just one thing" Tumbler pointed in the distance towards Annakus who was just sitting on the ground, legs crossed like a little girl listening to a story being told by her parents at bedtime, it was an eery sight to see, she had no expression, she was just taking it all in so she could relive the moment over and over again for her own amusement, seeing all these people suffering made her forget about the years of suffering she had endured while she searched for what she saw as her redemption...The Pieces.

Suddenly from nowhere Tumbler was pulled to the ground and dragged over the edge of the terrace, Sledge reached out to grab his hand but was too slow and Tumbler bounced off the rocks like a rag doll, his foot was attached to what Sledge could only describe as a pink, fleshy appendage, at the other end he could see the open month of Pishtaco, it was a man's face but a face that looked both alive and dead at the same time, zombie looking with dark sunken eyes and prominent check bones, its hair was dark and matted in congealed blood and it was dragging Tumbler closer and closer, Tumblers eyes were wide, his skin was pale and he was screaming at Sledge, "Help me, get this thing off me", his shoe fell off and for a minute Pishtaco lost its grip but as quick as it lost its grip it regained it around Tumblers now naked foot, small teeth dug into his ankle from the end of its proboscis, Tumbler yelled in pain as he could fell the fat being drained from his leg, Sledge saw his opportunity and lunged for Pishtaco, his massive body launched over the writhing Tumbler and slammed to the ground just in front of Pishtaco and with one slice he severed the proboscis clean off detaching it from Pishtacos open mouth and releasing Tumbler from its grip, the proboscis twitched for a moment before lying motionless on the ground, Pishtaco dropped of the ledge of the terrace and thrashed around on the floor for what seemed likes ages and finally stopped.

Tumbler grabbed Sledge's hand and Sledge sat him up against the wall, blood was oozing from the wound of his ankle and Sledge wrapped his belt around his ankle and pulled it tight, Tumbler winched, and the pain rushed through his whole body, he passed out.

Twenty minutes past before Tumbler finally came round, he was looking at the sky as Sledge dressed his wound, "Is it dead?"

Sledge looked down at him, "As far as I know, yes, it dropped over the edge of the terrace, so I assume it's dead but the way that thing was dragging you off anything is possible."

"And what about Annakus, any sign of her?" asked Tumbler.

"Not seen her, probably done her usual vanishing act" frowned Sledge.

Tumbler looked in the direction of the Intihuatana stone, he could see the sky above it was glowing green and knew Annakus was only two Pieces away from fulfilling her goal, then the pain rushed through his leg again and just before he passed out again, he muttered "India" then his eyes closed, and he was gone again.

Sledge thought about that word for a minute and put two and two together, "I guess that's where we are going next" he thought to himself, he picked up Tumbler in his arms and carried him to the coach full of panicking tourists, he managed to push his way through to the back of the coach and laid Tumbler down on the seat next to him, he could see the coach driver pushing people off and forcing the doors closed, the engine started and they were off.

The next time Tumbler woke he was back on the train then he drifted off again and then when he came around again, he sat in the departure lounge of Jorge Chávez International Airport.

"Thank god your awake!" sighed Sledge, "guess we are off to India now?

Tumbler looked puzzled "How do you know that?"

"It was the last thing you said before passing out at Machu Picchu.

"Oh right" said Tumbler "Yes we have to get to India, the next Piece is located at the Taj Mahal, it's the 6th Wonder, problem is it takes 26 hrs including transfers to get from Peru to India".

Sledge gasped "26hrs, well that's it then we are stuffed, we are already 5hrs down since Annakus placed the 5th Piece so have 19hrs left before she places the 6th, we won't get there in time to stop her", he threw his bag to the ground and paced backwards and forwards, trying to think of a solution but nothing.

Then Tumbler reached into his pocket and opened his hand, "We could give this a try" in his hand was the Iter stone.

Sledge looked at him puzzled "But you said it only transports 1 person, you can't do it alone".

"Who said I was going alone" Tumbler continued "It has only ever been done by one person, its only ever been one person protecting the Pieces so no Protector of the Septem has ever needed to try transporting two people, as long as it has a full charge then it should in theory be able to allow us both to travel but it will use all its power and there is a chance it may never recharge again but under the circumstances its worth a try isn't it" he raised his eyebrows and looked at Sledge.

"Well yes I suppose" frowned Sledge "But what if it doesn't work?

"If it doesn't work then it was nice knowing you and thanks in advance for your help" grinned Tumbler.

"What!" Sledge bellowed.

Tumbler giggled like a schoolchild, "I'm joking, it will be fine, the stone has the power to do it and I am only small anyway, if you carry me then we are connected enough for it to believe it is transporting one person."

Sledge shook his head in disapproval of Tumblers joke and lifted him into his arms, "Is it going to" but before he could finish talking Tumbler squeezed the Iter stone in his hand and the airport was gone, all Sledge could see was colours flashing past him, the was nothing below him, nothing above him, just purples, reds, yellows and greens, he had never seen so many colours and before he knew it they were on solid ground again, a Tok drove past them, then another, they were in the middle of the road surrounded by thousands upon thousands of pedestrians rushing in and out of the market stalls, carrying on with their daily business not paying any attention to the 6ft tall, red haired Scotsman carrying a small fat person, this was India and the next stage of their quest.

Chapter 14

"Yahmi" said Tumbler to himself still trying to remember what that word meant but his concentration was broken by a bellowing Scottish voice on the other side of the road "Come on we haven't got all day."

Delhi was massive with an estimated population of over 30 million people, Tumbler moved his way through the pedestrians and onto the road narrowly missing a car that was weaving in and out of the hundreds of vehicles littering the road, horns were sounding everywhere, it was mayhem, he finally made his way to Sledge who was stood next to a market stall selling fish, the stall next to it was selling herbs and spices and the one next to that was selling brightly coloured materials, each vendor was beckoning potential customers over to look at their merchandise and one wrapped a long piece of silk around Sledges chest "you wear this, it matches your beard" he grinned at Sledge and held his hand out, Sledge politely declined and handed the silk back to the vendor who was not pleased and stood behind his stall looking at Sledge through narrowed eyes, "see your making friends already" smirked Tumbler who somehow had managed to buy 2 Pink perch from the fish vendor next to them, "What are you going to do with those?" Sledge pointed at Tumblers bag of fish, Tumbler simply answered by handing the bag to the first person that walked past him, the guy looked at the little fat man, looked at the bag of fish, smiled and carried on with his day, "That's what I am doing with that" he grinned at Sledge and started walking in the opposite direction.

They made their way down the narrow, littered pavement trying to avoid the rushing locals, above their heads the buildings were covered in advertising and thousands of wires ran from one building to the next looking like a spider had spun a web of electric cables whilst the locals got on with their day to day lives, the thing that stood out to Sledge was the array of colours and although the streets were dirty, the buildings popped with colour not only from the posters and signs but from the silks and clothes that were hung in the open shop fronts, the women all wearing brightly coloured saris in all colours of the rainbow and some colours that he never knew existed, the men wore a more plain coloured dhoti wrapped around their waist and down to their ankles and Sledge thought maybe this is why the women's saris stood out even more, he was mesmerised.

A few minutes past and Sledge rounded a corner onto another street that looked exactly like the last when suddenly someone bumped into him and without looking at Sledge the person responded "'anā 'āsef", the word seemed to stand out from all the noise around him and Sledge turned his head into the direction it came from, he didn't catch the full face of the person as it was covered by a hood but he did notice one thing, the mysterious person had a green nose and cheek, he turned to Tumbler who he thought had been following him but was nowhere to be seen, he shouted at the top of his voice "Tumbler, TUMBLER" but no reply, the locals looked at him in confusion and went on their way apart from one boy, he was grubby looking with matted hair and scruffy clothes, he had no shoes on and his feet were black with dirt, he made his way over to Sledge and tried to make conversation, Sledge didn't notice him at first until the boy pulled on his sleeve, he held out his hand and Sledge placed one rupee into his open palm without even looking at him, suddenly he felt a tug again and as he looked down the boy was gone and then he noticed his bag was open and the Dirk was gone, he panicked and put his bag on the ground in front of him, he rummaged frantically through his belongings in case it had slipped down the side or was wrapped up in his dirty clothes, it was not there, he looked over the crowd and saw the boy climb up a drain pipe and onto a flat roof and then he saw a glint in his hand, it was the Dirk, Sledge threw his bag over his shoulder and bounded in the direction of the boy, he grabbed the drain pipe to follow him but it came away from the wall and Sledge fell onto his back, he watched the boy hop over the narrow gaps between the buildings as he pursued him along the street, the boy dropped off the roof onto a market stall below and back into the street, Sledge reached to grab him but the boy was too quick and he darted into an indoor market, Sledge scanned the crowd but the boy was nowhere to be seen, he made his way deeper into the market and just as he was about to give up he spotted him in a dark corner with a man, the boy handed the man the Dirk, he inspected it for a few moments and placed a few coins into the boys grubby trouser pocket, Sledge slowly moved in their direction and the boy disappeared into the crowd but the man stayed put inspecting his new acquisition then suddenly the man felt a hand around his throat, "I'll have that" said the deep Scottish voice and pulled the Dirk out of the man's hand, suddenly from nowhere the man shouted "ha madad" in Hindi and then again in English "Help" , people looked in the direction of the man being held around the throat by a pale, ginger haired Sledge, the man shouted again "chura lenevaala" once again in Hindi and then repeated himself in English "Thief", Sledge looked confused, he was not the thief the man was but the crowd didn't know that, he then saw 3 men in sand coloured uniforms and hats running towards him shouting "Stop", he glanced at the badges on their shirts, it was the Indian police or more commonly known by the locals as "Thulla", they grabbed Sledge and one took the Dirk out of his hand whilst the other grabbed his bag, one look in the bag and the policeman handcuffed Sledge and they escorted him out of the market and straight to the local police station, they threw him in a cell and took his bag into another room, Sledge sat down, head in his hands and just sighed, "shit" was the only word that came out of his mouth for a whole hour until he heard that familiar voice "What the F have you done?", Sledge looked up and saw Tumbler staring at him through the bars shaking his head.

He walked up to the bars and held them tight with his massive, cracked hands as if he was going to attempt to pull them apart and make a break for it, "What am I going to do now?" whispered Sledge to Tumbler, "I'm trying to work that out but how did you end up in here? enquired Tumbler shaking his head again like a disappointed father addressing his son.

"I was minding my own business trying to figure out where the hell you had vanished too when this little shit, street urchin stole the dirk out of my bag and legged it, I followed him into a market and found him selling it to this bloke, I grabbed the guy and he started yelling and then I ended up here".

Chapter 15

Just as Tumbler was about to shake his head at Sledge for the third time he heard a commotion coming from the office behind him, he moved closer and through the open door he could see a TV showing an breaking news bulletin, he couldn't quite hear what the reporter was saying but the looks on the police officers faces told him everything he needed to know, their faces where frozen with shock, there was a live link on the news, it showed a new reporter standing at the Great Gate that leads to the Taj Mahal, Tumbler squinted to make out the image of the historic building and suddenly noticed that one of the four minarets that adorn the four corners of the main mausoleum was lying in ruins, he flicked his eyes away for a moment to a clock that was hanging on the wall next to the TV, 4:01pm, suddenly out of the corner of his eye he saw something dark leap into the air behind the building and crash back down into the river, a massive wave smashed into the walls and the reporter dropped her microphone and fell to her knees, her face changed from shock to fear, he turned to Sledge who was still standing next to the bars trying to figure out what the commotion was all about when he suddenly heard sirens and police running from all directions, phones were ringing off the hook, Tumbler saw his opportunity and grabbed the keys to the cell off the desk in the now empty office, he threw them to Sledge who fumbled with the bunch of keys and eventually found the one that unlocked his cell door, "Oh hell no" he shouted at Tumbler "She's there, we need to get there quick".

"There is no quick about it" said a worried Tumbler, "it takes just over 3hrs to get to the Taj Mahal from Delhi and its already 4:10pm, we will never get there, we can't stop it, the doorway has opened and whatever that was that leapt out of the river has already come through, we just need to get there as soon as we can and hope for the best, Annakis will be gone too I bet but we can't just leave without trying to help somehow, can you drive a car?".

"I've drove my father's truck once" Sledge paused for a moment "but I was 10 years old and he changed the gears and worked the pedals, all I did was steer".

"We don't have time" declared Tumbler and he rushed out of the police station shortly followed by a bounding Sledge carrying his bag he had swiped out of the evidence locker on the way out, Tumbler jumped into the first taxi he could find, threw the driver the equivalent of a week's wages and told him to drive to the Taj Mahal and quick, the taxi driver couldn't believe his luck, he didn't say a word and slammed his foot on the accelerator and they were off, "Do you speak English" he asked the driver, "Yes I do sir, do you know something about what is happening at the Taj?", "You could say that we know a lot of what is going on and that is why we need to get there quick" replied Sledge "What are they saying on the radio", the taxi driver turned it up and said to Sledge in a soft, voice "They are saying that the fourth minaret has fallen and the sky has turned green".

Sledge looked at Tumbler, he was sitting next to the window just staring into space, he was picking his nails and rolling the Iter stones in his other hand, "Why didn't we use those?" Sledge pointed at the Iter stones, "We can't" replied Tumbler, "We used all the power they had getting to India; I don't even know if they will work again, they are still ice cold and if they do charge back up, we will know as they will be warm to the touch."

Suddenly the taxi driver turned his head and stopped the taxi, "What are you doing?" shouted Tumbler, the taxi driver turned the radio up again, "They say that the River Yamuna has burst its banks, giant waves caused the minarets to tumble and the Taj is slowly flooding, a creature was seen diving below the surface but that's as much detail they have of the creature", he started the taxi up again and started driving, "We will be there in just over an hour, I hope the Taj is still there!"

"What could be causing the waves?" Sledge asked Tumbler who had casted his memory back to the TV in the police station and then from nowhere he shouted "Timingila, Sledge looked at him surprised "Who or what is Timingila?" but before his friend could answer the taxi driver replied without taking his eyes off the road "Timingila is a giant aquatic creature like a shark that is so big that stories have been told of it swallowing Whales and it causes waves whilst hunting, I have heard the stories as a child but it's not real", Sledge looked at the taxi driver and simply said "I'm guessing it must be real based on the facts".

They sat back in the taxi watching the clock for what seemed like eternity when the silence was broken, Sledge nudged Tumbler, "I forgot to tell you, just before the boy stole my Dirk I was wondering the streets looking for you and someone bumped into me", Tumbler looked at him funny "So what, it's a busy place!", Sledge continued "No it's not that it's what they said", Tumbler narrowed his eyes, "What did they say?", Sledge thought for a moment trying to remember how to pronounce the word, at a few moments

he said "I know, they said ʾanā ʾāsef", Tumbler sat bolt

upright in his seat "ʾanā ʾāsef means sorry in Arabic, what did this person look like?", Well that's the weird bit, I could only see their head, it was covered with a hood but the nose and check was green, odd eh!", "what colour was the hood" asked Tumbler but before Sledge could answer Tumbler answered his own question, "It was Purple and Green wasn't it?", Sledge looked at him oddly for a few moments then replied "How do you know that?", Tumblers brow wrinkled "They have been following us for quite some time but I don't know why, I saw them by the kiosk in Wadi Musa before we got to Petra and again in the airport in Mexico before we reached Chichen Itza, I don't know who they are and can't figure out if they are friend or foe, I suppose only time will tell" he scratched his head and went back to staring out of the window, thoughts buzzed through his head like bees in a hive.

Time seemed to slow down for the pair and it felt like they were never going to make it, Tumbler looked at the clock on the dashboard, 6:55pm, they pulled up at the main gateway, Darwaza or Great Gate and thanked the driver, Tumbler threw him some more money for his trouble and they stood in front of the gateway, it was silent, Tumbler looked at the calligraphy on the Great Gate and read it out loud to Sledge "O Soul, thou art at rest. Return to the lord at peace with him, and he at peace with you" Sledge turned to Tumbler "Ironic I suppose based on the fact that all 4 columns now have come to rest in a pile of rubble but I don't feel much peace with the lord or him with what's just happened", Tumbler said nothing and they made their way through the garden towards the main mausoleum built by the Mughal emperor Shah Jahan to house the tomb of his favourite wife Mumtaz Mahal, the water had subsided but the river was still smashing waves again the bank and then Tumbler noticed that the dome on top of the mausoleum had also collapsed, his heart sunk and all he could see was bodies lying amongst the rubble, cameras strewn around the motionless tourists and weeds from the river draped over the remaining white marble that was once the great Taj Mahal, Sledge saw the Wonder piece glowing brightly in the side of Mumtaz Mahal's tomb and without thinking tried grabbing it out of its resting place, he threw his hand back and yelled in pain, the Piece was so hot that it burnt straight through his leather glove and left a small mark on his weathered palm, "Bollocks that hurt a wee bit", he shook his hand as if he was trying to swat a fly.

"It's been in there too long" replied Tumbler "You will never pull it out , She's bloody gone and done it this time, I wouldn't be surprised if she didn't set up that boy in the market to steel from you knowing that you would get thrown into jail, she will be long gone now and we have no way of stopping the Timingila, the River Yamuna is the second largest tributary of the Ganga and stretches 1376km, it could be anywhere by now, we have failed here but we can still try and stop the last Wonder stone from making it to its destination"

Sledge wrapped his hand in a dirty rag he found in his bag "And where is that or am I going to regret asking."

"Brazil," replied Tumbler, "Brazil" screamed Sledge.

"Yep Brazil, Christ the redeemer, the newest of the New seven wonders and the final resting place of the last Wonder Piece, the next problem is there is no direct flight to Brazil so it takes 24hrs to get there however Rio de Janeiro is roughly 8 and half hours behind Delhi, so if its 7:15pm then it will be 10:45am when we land so still giving us just enough time to get to the location and hopefully stop Annakus placing the last and most important Piece".

"Well let's get going" said Sledge and off they set on what could be the last chance to stop Annakus.

Chapter 16

It was just after 11am when the pair stepped off the plane at Galeao Airport, the sun was shining and the temperature was about to hit a manageable 26°C, the airport was right by the sea and Sledge could feel a slight breeze brushing across his face, he breathed in the sea air as his beard gently blew in the wind, he wiped a small bead of sweat off the end of his nose, the air smelt fresh and for a moment he forgot why he was there, that was until Tumbler rushed past him and reminded him they didn't have long and they made their way to the centre of Rio.

Sledge was hungry as always and looked around for somewhere to grab a bite to eat, he had been reading a magazine on the plane and had caught an article on foods from around the world, it happened that Brazil was mentioned, he fancied trying Empadão which is basically a chicken pie with a flaky crust, **filled with casseroled chicken** and a mix of vegetables such as corn, hearts of palm, and peas, he glanced around until he saw the word on a menu and went straight in and got one, he demolished it in three bites and went back for a second, Tumbler just looked at him and shook his head, "What?" said Sledge still chewing his final mouthful, "Oh nothing" replied Tumbler and turned heading towards a small stand advertising "Trips to the Lord", he moved closer and saw a small man waving at him wearing a short sleeved shirt and khaki linen shorts, "Next tour in an hour, I'll take you up close and personal with our lord Jesus Christ", Tumbler smiled and waved back at him "That would be fantastic" he shouted back but as he moved closer the man's face changed, his eyes were wide and he dropped to his knees, a women standing near him screamed and as she turned her face was covered in blood, the man slumped to the floor, Tumbler rushed over to his lifeless body and saw a small knife protruding from his neck, he stood up and looked at the crowd gathering around the local tour guide and spotted a familiar figure standing at the back, it was Annakus, she turned and headed away from the commotion, Tumbler tried to push past the people but by the time he reached the outside of the crowd she was long gone.

The women ran back over to the body of the tour guide and cradled his head in her lap, tears ran down her cheeks as blood gurgled from his mouth, he was trying to speak but it was faint, she moved her ear closer to the man and she could make out just two of the words he was trying to say "I love..." and that was it, he was gone, the women scream "No Jose, please don't leave me, Jose please", she brushed his black hair across his forehead and moved her hand gently over his eyes, she then slowly lowered his head onto the ground and lay hers on his chest, she closed her eyes and wept uncontrollably, Tumbler moved closer and knelt down next to her "My name is Tumbler, I am so sorry for your loss and I can assure you we will catch the women that done this", the women opened her eyes and looked at the small man now kneeling beside her, "are you Polícia? She said through her sobbing, "No but we know the women that did this", replied Sledge and just as Sledge was about to give the women his condolences she stood bolt upright with anger in her face, "You know her?" she shouted loudly beating her fists on Sledges chest, "You know the women who killed my Jose",

Sledge looked down at the pretty, black haired women, her olive skin catching the sun just right that it looked breath-taking, "Yes we do but not for good reasons, we are tracking her and have been for a while, we need to get to Christ the Redeemer before she does".

Just as the women was about to respond the local Police arrived with an ambulance in close pursuit, they took the women to one side as the ambulance crew loaded Jose's body onto a stretcher and covered him with a sheet, the Police started dispersing the crowd and some began asking the onlookers questions, trying to paint a picture of what had happened and by whom, Tumbler turned to Sledge, "We need to move, we don't want to get tied up in all this right now" he headed towards the women who was now sitting in the back of one of the Police cars, "how can we get to the Redeemer?" she looked at him with her large, brown eyes, the whites blood shot from all the crying, "You must find Carlos, he is Jose's brother, he runs a bar about 20 minutes from here called Pelé's Place, he can help you, tell him Adriana sent you", Tumbler took Adriana's hand and smiled at her "Thank you, We are sorry for you loss and will do everything we can", Adriana smiled back "You get the bitch".

The pair turned and headed in the direction that Adriana had pointed, they walked down the street that ran adjacent to the beach and in front of them they could make out a big green Neon sign that read "Pelé's Place", there were Brazilian flags hanging on both sides of the sign and a Brazilian football shirt hanging in the front window, it was a Sports bar, Sledge grinned from ear to ear, he was an avid Celtic fan and loved every sport imaginable but Tumbler did not match his enthusiasm, they stepped into the bar, it was covered in football memorabilia all dedicated to the great Pelé, a framed signed shirt hung next to a massive TV playing Pelé's 1970 World cup final match in which Brazil beat Italy 4-1, a photo of him being held aloft by his team mates hung on the other side of the TV, there was lots of other Sporting memorabilia adorning the walls, Volleyball and Basketball to name a few but it was 95% Football related, they walked up to the bar where a man was standing organising the spirits and wiping down the shelves, "Ola" said Tumbler in his best Portuguese accent, the man turned and looked at the odd man standing on the other side of the bar and then looked over at Sledge "Merda, seu grande" he said looking at Sledge with wide eyes, Sledge looked down at Tumbler, "What did he say?" and just before Tumbler could answer another man walked through a door at the back of the bar carrying a case of Caipirinha, a 30% proof liquor that is mixed with a little sugar and a piece of lime, "he said Shit your big, what can I do for you?".

"Carlos?" Tumbler said with an air of caution in his voice, "Yes" replied Carlos in English with a Portuguese twang, "who are you guys and how do you know my name?", "Adriana sent us, she said you could help us, we are trying to get to Christ the Redeemer", Carlos looked at them puzzled, "Why would Adriana tell you to find me, Jose is the tour guide, you would think his own wife would know this", he turned and put the crate down on the floor and started putting the bottles on the shelf that other man had just cleaned, "He's dead" Sledge blurted out, Tumbler looked at him in shook, "You could have been a little more subtle", Carlos turned to Sledge and said nothing, time seemed to stand still for a moment and the Carlos look down at Tumbler and softly asked "How?", Tumbler sat on the bar stool in front of him and explained to Carlos about Annakus and how Adriana had said that he could help, Carlos poured 3 glasses of Caipirinha and knocked his back, Sledge followed and Tumbler shortly after, coughing as he swallowed, Sledge held his hand up, "I'll take another one of those", Carlos poured another and slide it over to Sledge who knocked this one back too, he went to pour Tumbler another but Tumbler held his hand over the top of his glass "I'm good thanks".

Carlos poured his 3rd glass of Caipirinha and looked at a photo of himself and Jose in front of the bar on its first day of opening, "18th July 2005, I was 25 years old and Jose was 30, he knew my passion was football and drinking" he smiled to himself "I decided a year before that I wanted to open a Sports bar and Jose supported me all the way, we used to come here when we were younger and the previous owner Pablo had been a friend of the family since we were really small, one day he was out fishing and fell overboard reeling in a Brazilian Sharp nose shark" he pointed over at the set of jaws still hanging on the wall from one of Pablo's earlier fishing trips next to a photo of him standing next to his boat "The Sunset", "Myself and Jose found out a few weeks after his death that he had left us the bar but Jose had set his sights on being a tour guide after his first trip up to the Statue of Christ the redeemer so I took on the bar and he is.." he paused and looked at the floor, "was a silent partner".

Carlos poured his fourth glass of Caipirinha, and Sledge joined him beginning to feel a little lightheaded, "So will you help us?" Sledge slurred a little but composed himself before Tumbler noticed, "Of course I will, Jose was my brother and he looked out for me, I will do anything for him and I need to do this for Adriana, we leave now", Carlos threw the keys to the bar to the man now wiping the tables and in Portuguese said "você está no comando, cuide dela para mim e lembre-se de fechar à meia-noite, Sledge looked at Tumbler with a confused look on his face, Carlos saw his confusion and smiled at the pair, "I told him that he is in charge and to remember to close at midnight, I've left him in charge before and the bar was still open at 8am and he was passed out on the bar, luckily we don't get much trouble and this is the first time I have left him in charge since that night".

The pair followed Carlos to the rear of the bar, there was a garage with a large door and they were not surprised when they saw a portrait of Pelé that had been painted over the top of a Brazilian flag, Carlos pulled up the door and inside was what looked like a car covered in a sheet, he pulled back the sheet to unveil a green and yellow 1953 VW Beetle known locally as a "Fusca", it had a little rust on the rear arches and a small spot on the bonnet but other than that it was beautiful, Tumbler loved cars although he couldn't drive he remembered a Karman Ghia he once rode in with his father, Carlos patted the car on the roof and whispered "Ola linda", Sledge looked at Carlos, "You called her Linda, not very Brazilian if you ask me", Carlos laughed "No linda means gorgeous in Portuguese, I said Hello gorgeous, I haven't driven her in 2 years, been too busy".

"She will start won't she" asked Sledge and then he heard the engine cough into life and Tumbler revelled in the sound of the engine purring, he closed his eyes and took it in for a minute before realising that Carlos and Sledge were already in the car, he jumped in, and they drove out of the garage and onto the streets of Rio.

Chapter 17

The trio took the road to the Paineiras car park halfway up the Corcovado mountain where they were greeted by a guy waving them into the car park, Carlos wound down his window and shook the man's hand, the man smiled "Hey Carlos, what are you doing up here, thought you would be on your second bottle of Caipirinha by now" he pointed at his watch, "And where is Jose, he has missed 3 tours already, I've had to send 4 taxis back already, have had a few hikers though", Carlos explained to the parking attendant what had happened to Jose, the parking attendant turned the sign on the car park entrance to closed for the first time in years, patted Carlos on the back through the open window and waved him on, just before they were about to drive on Tumbler wound down his window and said to the guy "Any of these hikers look peculiar to you?", the parking attendant thought for a moment and looked at the little man leaning out of the back window of the VW, "Come to think about it there was a women I thought looked a little oddly dressed to be hiking", Tumblers eyes widened, "Was she wearing a black dress and carrying a leather satchel with a number 7 on the front!", "Yes she was" replied the attendant, "Friend of yours?", Tumbler looked at the dusty road below him and replied with an air of disappointment in his voice, "Family, how long ago did you see her", "Oh about an hour or so, grumpy lady, was in a hurry to get to the top" remarked the attendant, "Oh and by the way there was another man, he was really odd, dressed in a green and purple dress wearing a green mask, didn't speak but his friend asked about the lady in black, funny little olive-skinned man he was", Tumbler looked at Sledge, reached over and tapped Carlos on the shoulder in a gesture indicating that he needed to hurry, as the car drove past him the attendant shouted "Send my love to Adriana", Carlos waved back and put his thumb up, wiping away a single tear from under his eye.

"whoever it is are here, who the hell is it and are they helping Annakus or trying to stop her" Tumbler tapped his fingers on the window as he tried to answer his own question, "I guess you're talking about the person in the green and purple Kaftan and green mask that bumped into me in Delhi" replied Sledge, "but who is the Olive-skinned man?", Tumbler was looking vacantly out of the window, brow wrinkled so much it was starting to hurt his head "yes I am, it's really odd, I can't figure it out" but just as he was about to continue his thinking was interrupted by the screeching of brakes, he leaned between the front seats, "What's going on Carlos, why did you stop so quick?", Carlos pointed and Tumbler could see why they had stopped, there were 3 trees laying across the road, slightly burned at the bottom, the pair looked at each other and at the same time yelled "Annakus", Carlos was startled for a moment, opened his driver's door and turned at the two still sitting in the car, "Well what are you waiting for, we walk from here, it's only around the corner.

Sledge grabbed his bag from the back seat and swung it over his shoulder, he unzipped it and pulled out a small knife and tucked it in his boot, "Fail to prepare and prepare to fail", Tumbler nodded "Got another" he asked with confidence in his voice, Sledge was a little taken back but reached in and grabbed out another, "Look after it, I don't go giving my knives away every 5 minutes", Tumbler took it and slipped it into his inside pocket next to the remaining flash stones and the Iter stones.

The 3 made their way up the road and as the rounded the corner there it was, standing 30 metres high, his white soapstone figure shining in the sunlight, arms spread out welcoming the world he is looking down on, Christ the Redeemer, the youngest, newest edition to the New seven wonders of the world and the final key to unlocking the Septem was standing right in front of them, crowds gasped at its size, people were reaching into the sky as if they were trying to get Christs attention, it was an amazing sight to see but not one that Tumbler and Sledge could enjoy for too long, suddenly they heard a scream from inside the statue and a loud thud, "Tumbler shrieked at Carlos, "How do you get in?", "You can't" replied Carlos, "The only people allowed in are the maintenance crew, there are wooden steps that lead to the head but it's not open to the public".

Suddenly from nowhere a middle-aged man in overalls came running through the doorway at the base of the statue yelling at the top of his voice, he was shaking uncontrollably, Carlos grabbed him by the shoulders and shook him, "Get a grip, what's wrong?", the man was stuttering his words, "ele está morto oh senhor ele está morto", Carlos replied in Portuguese and again in English for the sake of his two companions, "Whose dead?", the man still shaking just said the person's name, "Luiz" and fell to his knees sobbing, "She kill him!".

Before they could ask the man anymore questions the ground shook, the door way at the base of the statue began to crumble and Sledge saw his opportunity, he threw his 6ft 4 frame through the doorway just as the frame collapsed, he felt around for a bit and put his hand into something soft, a small bead of light was shining through a crack in the crumbled doorway and he could just make out feet, he felt around some more and put his other hand in something wet, he put his hand up to the light and could see red, it was blood, "I think I have found Luiz" he muttered to himself and reached into his bag and pulled out a small flash light, he shone it on the ground and was greeted by the mangled mess of a man in overalls, harness still around his waist and a short bit of rope that had been cut still attached to it with a karabiner, his helmet was cracked and blood was running out onto the ground surrounding his lifeless body.

Sledge grabbed the wooden hand rail and made his way up the stairs, he was about halfway up when he felt another shudder and one of the steps gave way plunging his right foot ground wards, he managed to pull it back up to the next step and was only 4 more steps up when he felt another shudder but this time more aggressive, he could hear voices shouting and screaming below him, he wasn't wearing a watch but he could guess what was occurring and then he saw it, the flash of green blinded him for a moment, he rubbed his eyes and could see an opening and a dark figure, the bottom half of its body inside the statue and the top half outside, arm stretched out towards the right hand side of Christs head, he grabbed at the figures foot, Annakus pulled away just in time and pulled herself outside onto Christs shoulder, Sledge reached the opening and just as he was about to move into the sunlight he felt a blow to the side of his head, it dazed him for a brief second, he ducked just in time before a second fist made contact with his temple, Annakus was holding on to a length of climbers rope attached by a single karabiner just below the statues neck, the rope that had secured Luiz before Annakus had cut it sending him plummeting to his death.

Watching the commotion from below Tumbler and Carlos were helpless, people were barging past them from all directions and some were stood pointing at the women in black stood high above their heads on Christs shoulder, Tumbler didn't notice the Olive-skinned man brush past him at first but suddenly realised his pocket felt heavier than it had a few moments earlier, he reached in and pulled out a small leather pouch with a drawstring top, he pulled open the pouch and inside he could make out what looked like red marbles, there were 6 in total and 1 single blue stone, the red marbles felt warm to the touch.

He scanned through his brain like a researcher in a library, trying to figure out where he had seen these before and suddenly hit dawned on him, 16th January 1864, Dandridge, Tennessee, the day the confederates had attacked the Unions troops, the day his father had died, his father Luka had used one of these to hold back the confederates, General William Sherman was amazed by the sheer fire power it had produce, as if the sun had exploded, they would throw smaller fragments off which would in turn explode causing whoever or whatever was attacking to retreat, Tumbler had forgot to mention this when he told the story of his father to Sledge back when they first met but now it was all coming back, they were called Repeater stones and more powerful than the stone that Tumbler had used at the Great wall against Shenlong however Tumbler couldn't work out what the single blue stone was or how someone had managed to get hold of them, but what he had worked out was this Olive-skinned man was a friend not a foe and knew more about the mission in hand than Tumbler had realised, but how?.

There wasn't time to contemplate as the ground shook again but this time the space below their feet started to crack, Carlos jumped to one side and Tumbler to the other as the Sky glowed green and the ground crumbled beneath them and then they saw it, fire leapt from the crack in the ground and from the fire a giant creature slithered out, narrowly missing Carlos by just a few feet, "What the hell is it?" he screamed at Tumbler, "Boitata, the Fire Snake" replied Tumbler, Carlos face turned white, "But it's a myth, a story, it's not real", he couldn't believe his eyes, Tumbler looked at him and with no expression on his face simply said "Well you better believe it and if you can keep your eyes closed that would help you too", Carlos looked puzzled then as he looked over his shoulder he remembered why from the stories he had been told from his childhood, a man with a video camera was recording the event as it unfolded but suddenly Boitata turned, flicked out her forked tongue and straight into the man's eye sockets, the man fell to his feet screaming in pain and Carlos could see his eye balls on the end of its tongue, it disappeared into Biotata's mouth and suddenly its skin glowed brighter, the more eyes it devoured the brighter it got and the brighter it got the stronger and bigger it grew, its tale flicked knocking one of Christs outstretched arms clean off sending it plummeting to the ground.

High above, Sledge was still battling with Annakus but the arm breaking off sent him falling through the hole, luckily he managed to grab a rung on the ladder as he fell, he pulled himself back up just as he saw Annakus with the rope in hand jump off the shoulder and swing to the ground below knocking a group of tourists into the trees below, she barrel rolled, stood and brushed off her dress, took one final look at what she had started and vanished, she had done it, she had completed the first part of her mission, all the pieces were in and now it was down to the finale, Sledge reached into his bag and pulled out the rope and grappling hook, he attached it to a small girder that was protruding from where the arm had been, closed his eyes and jumped, he swung around Christs waist like Tarzan letting out a booming yell as he knocked into one of the large feet and dropped the final 6ft to the floor, he regrouped and made his way to Carlos and Tumbler jumping over Boitata's writhing tail ,Tumbler looked at Sledge, "Thanks for joining us, finished playing?", Sledge didn't reply.

People were rushing everywhere, some holding their faces where their eyes had been, some with one hand covering their face and some just screaming on the floor, the lucky ones were making their way down the road, retreating back to the car park leaving their belonging scattered all over the floor and all the time this was happening Boitata grew brighter and stronger, Sledge remembered how he had stopped Shenlong back in China but Boitata was bigger and more powerful, the rope trick wasn't going to work for a second time so he had to come up with another plan and fast.

Sledge scanned his surroundings for anything he could use to help, Biotata flicked her head round and spotted the Scotsman reaching into his bag but before he could pull anything out she swung her tail around and launched Sledge into the air, he landed on his side which took his breath away, he tried reaching into his bag once again but this time felt a sharp pain in his right shoulder, it was dislocated and bad, he knew this as he had injured the same shoulder a few years back whilst playing football for Killington FC, a rare occasion when he wasn't working in the forge.

He stood up and winched as she swung her tail again, once again knocking Sledge to the ground on the same side, his face twisted with agony, he he saw Carlos running full speed in his direction swinging what looked like a chain around his head, on closer inspection Sledge could see it was indeed a chain and one used to close the queuing area at the end of the day, Carlos swung it again and let go striking Biotata underneath he massive jaw, it gave Sledge time to collect himself and make his way towards the car park, his right shoulder dropped lower than his left.

Sledge reached the car park closely followed by Carlos, he turned to Carlos and shouted "Throw me your keys!", Carlos looked at him "What?, Why?", Sledge didn't have time to explain, "just throw me your god damn keys!", Carlos reached into his pocket and retrieved the keys to the VW, he threw them at Sledge, "Please be careful with her" and although Carlos had begged Sledge to do so he had a feeling at the pit of his stomach he didn't like the feel of.

Sledge looked around and found the closest tree he could find and slammed his right shoulder into it, it crunched, echoed through the hills and popped back into place, Sledge screamed in pain, Carlos was nearly sick when he heard the noise, then he saw Sledge open the door to the VW, put the keys in the ignition and rev the hell out of the engine, all Carlos could think was "Oh my baby!".

During this Biotata was rapidly making her way closer to the pair, Tumbler was nowhere to be seen but there was no time to worry about him, he could look after himself, Sledge unscrewed the fuel cover and pushed one of his dirty shirts deep into the tank with just a small part sticking out, Biotata lowered her head towards the road and level with the VW, Sledge saw an opportunity, he plunged his hand into his pocket and pulled out a zippo lighter and with a few clicks lit the end of his shirt.

He slammed his foot on the accelerator pedal, pushed the gearstick into first gear and wheel spun in the gravel, he sped past Carlos in the direction of an angry Biotata who had opened her mouth, her large forked tongue now on the road, Sledge looked in the wing mirror, he could see the shirt ablaze and just as he was nearing the tip of her tongue he opened the door and rolled out onto the gravel road taking some of the shin off his elbow with it, the VW clipped Biotata's tongue and flipped into the back of her throat, Carlos watched in disbelief as his beloved car disappeared, she thrashed her head around trying to dislodge the VW and suddenly the flames that where flicking from Sledges old shirt vanished into the tank, a rumbling sound emitted from inside the VW and then it happened, a massive explosion, Biotata raised her scaley red body high into the air and shards of metal flew in all direction, some from her mouth and some sliced through her thick skin at the corners of her mouth, part of her jaw dropped as the bone shattered, above him Carlos heard a whistle, he looked up and dived to his right, he heard a crash just yards from his head, he rolled to one side and looked in the direction of the crash, he could see a green and yellow piece of metal, on closer inspection he figured out what it was, it was what used to be the bonnet of his VW Beetle, the remains of his pride and joy lay twisted at his feet, he looked at Sledge then looked at Biotata, she was writhing around the road, head knocking into trees and uprooting them, her jaw was hanging off and part of her tongue was missing, Carlos moved closer, Sledge screamed at him "No Carlos, back off!, Carlos turned his head to one side but before he could acknowledge Sledge Biotata plunged the remaining fork of her tongue into Carlos's right eye socket, Carlos rolled on the floor, the pain was excruciating like someone had pushed a hot spike into his head, he got to his feet covering the hole where his eye had been and ran to a camper van in the car park that had been abandoned by its owners who were now long gone or dead, he didn't know, all he knew was he had to get somewhere safe, he hot-wired the van and made his way towards Sledge, "Get in" he bellowed at Sledge but Sledge waved him on, "Get to safety, get that wound looked at, I'm going to find Tumbler" and with that Carlos drove back down the road towards the town.

Tumbler looked around trying to find his friends but could see nothing but dead or crippled bodies, then he spotted him, the Olive-skinned man was cowering under the remnants of Christs fallen arm, Tumbler grabbed his shirt and pulled him out "Who are you?", the Olive-skinned man said nothing, he tried again "Who are you?" this time grabbing his shirt with both hands, the Olive-skinned man held up his hands, the fingers on his left hand were bruised and deformed and 2 looked broken, "I not say, I am friend", Tumbler looked at him oddly, "How do you know me?", the Olive-skinned man stood up, "I not know you, Master know who you are, he help", Tumblers eyes narrowed "The man in the green and purple kaftan wearing the green mask is your master, but who is he?", the olive-skinned man's eyes closed for a moment and just before he could answer and familiar figure appeared in the distance, it was Annakus, Tumbler looked back in the direction of the olive-skinned man but he was gone, he had vanished into thin air, Tumbler was fuming as he was seconds away from learning the identity of his anonymous supporter but his attention was now drawn towards Annakus, they faced each other, the only thing in their way was the broken arm of Christ, Annakus glared at Tumbler with her black, sunken eyes, "You thought you could stop me, you and your stupid red haired friend but you were wrong, I am powerful, I am the destroyer of the Septem and no one gets in my way!", Tumbler screamed back at her, "You have nothing to gain, you are just killing innocent people, destroying lives and for what?, to get back at your father for not trusting you, surely there are better ways to deal with this?", Annakus ignored Tumblers plea, "You don't understand, you never will, I will destroy the Septem and show him he shouldn't have messed with me", She raised her arms into the air, the sky above her still a brilliant green, he long black hair blowing in the breeze, "Fear the Destroyer of the Septem, bow down to me and watch your planet burn" and with that she was gone.

Tumbler turned and, in the distance, he could see the outline of Boitata and then he spotted Sledge moving slowly towards him holding his right shoulder and sporting a bloody elbow, he could see Boitata's jaw and the remains of Carlos's VW scattered around the road, he kicked a motionless Biotata with his small leather boots, he looked at Sledge and before he could ask him a question Sledge simply said "Don't ask!",

Tumbler had his back to Boitata when suddenly Sledge grabbed his shirt and pulled him away as Boitata's head lifted for a moment and slammed back to the ground, there was the sound of air rushing from her lungs and finally nothing.

People gathered, mouths wide open at the site of the mythical creature, camera flashes where lighting up the scene and 2 news channel vans screeched up beside Sledge and the reporters jumped out, each one trying to get the best shot and motioning to the camera man to start filming, Sledge and Tumbler saw an opportunity to slip away before they got wrapped up in the carnival they had created.

Chapter 18

They reached Peles Place and saw the TV on the wall playing Channel 49, one of the news reporters stood in front of Biotata whilst a tall, Brazilian backpacker posed for the camera, one foot on the ground, the other resting on what was left of her jaw, he had a massive grin on his face and his hands were on his hips as he had just defeated the beast, Sledge and Tumbler laughed to each other and made their way to the bar, from the back room they could hear the bartender talking to someone on the telephone, they couldn't make out what they were saying as he was talking Portuguese however they did make out the name Adriana and Carlos.

The phone call ended, and the bartender strolled out from the back room with a half empty bottle in one hand and 3 empty shot glasses in the other, he said nothing, he just poured three shots and slide 2 over to Tumbler and Sledge, they knocked them back in sync with each other and Tumbler spluttered as the liquid hit the back of his throat, "Any news on Carlos?" Tumbler attempted some Portuguese, but the bartender looked at him blankly and smiled, just then the bar door flew open, and Adriana ran up to Sledge and wrapped her arms around his massive waist, "You saved Carlos, I couldn't lose Jose and Carlos in the same day!", Sledge wasn't sure what to do so he just patted her on the back and with a calming tone just said, "No worries".

Tumbler approached Adriana, "How is Carlos, any news?", Adriana poured herself a shot and replied, "He is going to be fine, going to be watching football out of his left eye only from now on and looks like a pirate but the main thing is he is safe thanks to your big, strong friend.", for the first time since meeting Sledge Tumbler saw him blush.

As they sat in the bar the News on the TV suddenly switch to another breaking news story, they pulled their stools closer and Adriana indicated with her fingers for the bartender to turn up the volume, Sledge and Tumbler looked at each other as the news-reporter spouted out what to them was gibberish but to the bartender and Adriana was as clear as day, "Oh my god!" Adriana had her hand over her mouth when she said it and then the screen split into seven, there was a news reporter at every location Sledge and Tumbler had been to, one next to the Great Wall of China, another by the Colosseum, one in Machu Picchu and so on, they all had panicked looks on their faces, however although the Wonder pieces still glowed they had now changed colour, their normal green glow was gone and replaced by a blood red beam shooting into the sky from the location of the Wonder pieces, it felt more ominous, Sledge stepped outside and called Tumbler out a few seconds later, they both looked in the direction of the Christ the Redeemer statue, they could see the red glow disappearing into the sky as if Christ was sending a signal to the heavens, Tumbler turned away, dropped to his knees and screamed and for the first time Sledge heard him curse "What the fuck have you done Annakus?" Sledge grabbed Tumbler's shoulder and pulled him to his feet, "This can't be over, there must be something we can do, think Tumbler, what would your father have done?" Tumbler put his head in his hands and pushed his thumbs against his temples as if he were trying to squeeze out memories buried deep from years and years ago.

Suddenly Adriana rushed out "You need to see this", the pair followed her back into the bar and she pointed at the TV, a reporter stood in front of the entrance to Petra had just cut to another breaking story by one of his Aljazeera colleagues, he was stood in front of the Pyramids, speaking so fast that Tumbler and Sledge really had to concentrate then as the shot zoomed out Tumbler remembered, "Giza" he shouted at the top of his voice, "Its Giza", Everyone looked at each other in astonishment, Adriana turned to Tumbler and put her hand on his shoulder "Everyone knows that's Giza", Tumbler looked frustrated "No you don't understand, that's what my father was trying to say before he died, I asked him who Gi was, Gi wasn't a person, he was trying to say Giza, that's Septem, that's what I've been protecting all these years, The Great Pyramid of Giza, the only remaining ancient Wonder of the world is the Septem.

They turned back to the TV still trying to process the news that Tumbler had just thrust upon them then suddenly the ground shook, the screen flickered and there was a massive flash of Red, the camera zoomed out once again and the camera man tried to steady the shot, they could see 6 blood red beams of light hitting different points of the Great pyramid like giant laser sight from a sniper rifle then suddenly a seventh hit the top of the pyramid like a lightning bolt, the reporter fell backwards in shock as the outer limestone shell of the Great pyramid began to crumble revealing a jaw dropping, beautiful Gold top with silver walls were the limestone and granite once lay, the silver walls reflecting the moonlight in all directions, it was spectacular but horrifying at the same time.

Then the Screen went black.

Chapter 19

"What the hell?" shouted Sledge, nothing, no one responded, everyone just stood there with their mouths wide open still trying to digest what had just happened, then suddenly Tumbler turned and ran out of the bar, Sledge had never seen him move so fast and struggled to keep up with him, Tumbler steeped into the street and put his hand out in front of him in a "Stop" motion, the oncoming traffic screeched to a holt, horns blasting, he made his way along the stationing cars and jumped in the back of the first taxi with no one in it, Sledge pushed in beside him, Tumbler screamed one word at the driver "Airport", the driver looked at him in disbelief and flicked the meter.

Just as the taxi was about to move off the passenger door opened, it was Carlos, Sledge and tumbler looked at him, then each other and back at him, "What are you doing?", Carlos looked at him with his good eye, "I'm coming with you, you never know I might have to save your life" he winked at Sledge, Sledge fist bumped him and the driver did a U-turn and headed for the airport.

"So how long do we have?" Carlos asked Tumbler, Tumbler looked out of the window at the statue of Christ the Redeemer, its blood red beacon shinning into the night sky, the road leading to it now a distant memory gone, the only reminder that there used to be a road was the cars strewn down the mountain side, "we have all the time in the world or what's left of it, it's not like the Wonder pieces where they activate after 24 hrs of the last, they are all active now, the destruction has begun and all we can do is minimise the damage, I still don't know what to expect when we get to Egypt but our only option now is to save humanity".

Sledge's stared at Tumbler, his eyes wide like an owl, he was repeating 5 words in his head that Tumbler had just said and then they came out of his mouth, "or what's left of it!, what do you means what's left of it?", "Well" began Tumbler "To put it in simple terms The Septem is the lock and the 7 Wonders are the combination like a safe, as each Wonder piece is placed it is like turning the dial on the safe to the first number and after the last number to the combination is put in it opens the lock" he points to the statue, "Then the door to the safe opens, the safe being The Septem".

Sledge looked at him, "I get that but what's in the Safe?" Tumbler hung his head "That I don't know but I know it's not good and whatever it is, it has the power to destroy the earth as we know it.

The radio in the taxi crackled and Carlos leaned forward and turn it up, he twisted his head to the rear of the car and repeated to his new friends what he had just heard, "They say that part of the Colosseum in Rome has collapsed, 250 people have died and another 50 wounded by falling rubble".

With this in their minds they pull up at the airport, they stepped into the empty departure lounge and stared up at the screens, the same word repeated on every flight "Cancelled" Tumbler ran towards a guy dressed in a Pilots uniform, he grabbed his sleeve, the guy looked at him "What are you doing" Tumbler looked at him wide eyed "We need to get to Egypt", the pilot laughed and in an American accent said "Do you not watch the news, you do know what the fuck is going on out there, the world is falling apart", "I gathered that!" Tumbler replied quite abruptly "I will pay."

The Pilot looked at the 3 guys stood in front of him, the one with the patch, the other with his big red beard and leather waistcoat and the little one, all looking like they had just come back from a weird convention, he took off his hat and ran his fingers through his hair, flicking his fringe to one side and tucking it back under his hat, "Look, I am not getting into the air for all the money in the world, there is crazy shit happening out there and you need someone who doesn't give a rats ass and that isn't me" he paused for a moment, "maybe, just maybe Tony is still in the hanger just off runway 4, he would do anything for bottle of whiskey let alone a bag of cash", Tumbler turned on his heals and ran as fast as his short legs could carry him, out of the door and towards the hanger on runway 4, Sledge smacked the pilot on the back so hard that he nearly knocked his hat off, "Cheers buddy, you get to safety" and no sooner had Sledge finished talking the pilot was gone.

Sledge and Carlos could see the Tumbler shaped figure bounding towards a massive arched hanger with huge double doors, the doors were slightly open and they could see a bead of light shining through the crack, they caught Tumbler up just as he walked through the open doors, "Hello" shouted Tumbler "Tony, are you in here?", they heard footsteps on metal and coming down the steps of a large private jet they could see a tall, slender-looking man in scruffy jeans, braces and an oily white t-shirt looking in their direction, the man dropped his glasses onto the bridge of is nose and in a strong Cockney accent replied "Who's asking?" Sledge spoke before Tumbler had the chance "I guess you are Tony, the American pilot we spoke to in the departure lounge told us to find you, we need to get to Egypt", Tony looked at the huge Scotsman and scratched his head, "Bloody hell, has that spineless wimp legged it, it's only a few earthquakes and a couple storms, what's to worry about and why do you 3 need to get to Egypt so fast, going to visit your mummy?", Tony laughed to himself but unfortunately Sledge didn't find it amusing, he grabbed Tony by his braces, "listen here smart ass, you have no clue what is actually going on and if you want to keep those braces attached to the waistband of your trousers and not something inside your trousers the I suggest you stop with the jokes and tell me, can you fly this thing?"

Tony, even though he was slim, still stood at eye level and was surprisingly strong grabbed Sledges wrist and squeezed "You better take your hands off me mate before I break your wrist and to answer your question, Yes I can fly this thing, been flying them for years so you want to be changing your attitude sonny Jim if you want my help", Tumbler tugged at Sledges sleeve and gestured to him to calm down, he looked at Tony, "If you could help it would be great, it's a matter of urgency" he threw Tony a small purse that was tied to his belt and Tony caught it in his left hand, he cupped the purse and moved his hand up and down as if he was weighing the contents, he opened it and his mouth dropped open "Shit me, looking at you I wouldn't of imagined you carry around this sort of thing" he poured the contents of the purse onto the toolbox sitting under the plane's wing and out fell 2 gold nuggets, "Where did you get these?" he asked Tumbler, Tumbler looked a t Sledge and smiled "Oh just a small family inheritance, will you help"?, Tony didn't hesitate to answer, "fuck yeah" he grinned pocketing the 2 gold nuggets, "What you waiting for jump aboard but keep that big red haired bastard away from me whilst I'm flying", Tumbler and Carlos acknowledged Tony's request and walked up the steps into the Gulfstream IV.

The 3 had never been in anything so elaborate, plush leather seats, a long sofa to one side and a table with 2 more chairs on the other, Carlos and Tumbler sat on the two chairs closest to the cockpit ensuring that they kept Tony's wish by seating Sledge as far away from him as possible, Sledge dumped his bag down next to the table and moved towards the bar, he leaned over and grabbed a bottle of Jack Daniels whiskey, unscrewed the cap and took a massive gulp, "I'll be over there if anyone wants me" and gestured towards the long sofa, he fell backwards onto it, plumped up the pillows and rested his large, dirty black boots onto the arm of the perfect, cream leather leaving black marks everywhere, Carlos looked at Tumbler who just shrugged his shoulders and closed his eyes.

It wasn't long before the engine of the Gulfstream roared into life, "hang on to your man parts it's going to be a bumpy ride" shouted Tony as he slammed the plane down the runway and pulled the nose up lifting them into the air, "Egypt here we come", Tony gave a crazy laugh and manoeuvred the plane gracefully through the cloudy night sky.

A few hours had passed and Sledge was now snoring his head off, one arm hanging off the edge of the sofa still holding onto a now empty bottle of Jack, Carlos got out of his chair and switched on the TV built into the planes wall, he flicked through the channels and everyone he stopped on was reporting live, he sat mesmerised as a Chinese reporter pointed to a large part of the Great wall, there was a 30 metre expanse of the wall missing, rubble lay strewn all around, people were running around hands on their heads, some covered in dust and debris, the camera spun around to show the blood red beam shooting high into the sky and through all of the commotion Carlos just made out the word Dragon and another word he wasn't sure he had heard correctly, he nudged Tumbler who jumped up from his chair were he had been peacefully sleeping in and stood bolt up-right, "What!" his voice trembling, Carlos apologised "Sorry, but who is Shenlong?", Tumbler looked puzzled for a moment, how did Carlos know about Shenlong, "Why do you ask?", Carlos didn't respond he just pointed at the TV screen, Tumbler squinted and suddenly he saw what looked like the tip of a green tail flick through the gap where part of the wall used to be, "That's not possible!, how?, what the hell!" "What's going on?" replied Carlos but Tumbler didn't have time to reply, he ran over to Sledge, forced his massive boots off the arm of the chair and shook him vigorously, "You did kill Shenlong back in China, please say you did!", Sledge looked at him through glazed eyes, "What are you talking about" he slurred, "Shenlong" Tumbler responded, "You did check she was dead didn't you?" Sledge thought for a moment, "She must have been, I slit her throat with the dagger, she fell to the floor, you were there too, I thought you checked!"

Tumbler slumped into the chair, arms hanging over the side as if he had given up, "I don't think she is dead, I'm sure I saw her tail on the News" Sledge was confused, "Your tired buddy, maybe you were just seeing things."

Whist all this was going on Carlos was licking through the channels again and stopped on one reporting from Chichen Itza, he called the pair over so they could watch too, the camera was pointing directly at the Pyramid of Kukulkan when suddenly something leaped towards the camera knocking it over, the camera lay on its side and something ran past, the camera started bumping along the ground and in one frame Sledge and Tumbler saw something very familiar indeed, they looked at each other and at exactly the same time said exactly the same thing "Alux", Carlos looked at them, "What is an Alux?", Sledge just shook his head, turned to Carlos and sighed "All you need to know is they are a bloody nightmare" he turned to Tumbler, "I don't get it, first Shenlong, now an Alux, what's happening?".

"It looks to me like the activation of the 7th doorway has awakened everything we thought we hand stopped, the creatures we thought we had defeated are being called by something, but I don't know what, but it must be something to do with Giza".

Chapter 20

Another hour past and the three sat watching the News unfold, every scene the News report flicked too showed carnage and mayhem, the death toll was rising and quickly, then the silence was broken by the voice of Tony, "Sorry to spoil your date night but we are about to land", "Which airport" asked Tumbler, "Airport" laughed Tony, "You said nothing about an airport, you just said Egypt and Giza, so you better buckle up, it's going to be a rough landing", on that note Tumbler pulled up one of the blinds on the window next to his seat and peered out, his eyes widened as he saw sand getting closer and closer, "quickly clipped his seat belt and shouted to Carlos and Sledge "He's landing in the god damned desert", Carlos looked panicked "how can he be landing, the landing gear hasn't come down yet", Tony shouted through the now open door of the cockpit "what's the point in wheels, we are landing in the bloody desert, haven't you ever been snowboarding?", Sledge growled at Tony "What the fuck has snowboarding got to do with the desert you crazy old bastard", Tony brushed off the insult "I'll land the plane on its belly, we will slide for a moment and then I will bring the nose gently down into the sand and job done, easy peasey".

The three braced themselves ready for what they expected to be their last few minutes, they felt the belly of the plane touch the sand, it slid along the desert like a snake, weaving from side to side and then they were thrown forward in their seats and the plane came to a crashing holt.

They unclipped and made their way to the cockpit, they could fell a breeze and when they walked through the door they stepped onto sand, they couldn't see Tony but then they heard him "Whoops", Tumbler could see the outline of Tony sitting on a dune "What do you mean whoops", Tony giggled like a looney "I may have broken the plane a tad, it's had a bit of a nose job but on a positive note, we are safe and sound on the penny a pound" What's he on about?" said Carlos, Tumbler shrugged, "Its cockney slang for ground" Sledge confirmed, he walked past Tony and just pointed his massive finger in his face "You're a nutcase, a fucking liability, you are not coming any further with us, I'm done with you", Tumbler steeped between Sledge and Tony, "The more hands the better" Tumbler quietly said to Sledge who just spun on his heels and grabbed his bag out of the now wreaked $26.2 million gulfstream that lay smoking and creaking in the scorched sand.

The temperature outside was 10°c and the time was around 2am but the sky wasn't black, it was a bright red, they could see the Great pyramid of Giza about a mile away, the 7 blood red beams reflecting off the silver walls of the pyramid then from nowhere a voice called out in broken English "Mr Tumbler, Mr Tumbler", Sledge stopped in his tracks, "Did you hear that, someone is calling your name Tumbler", they all stopped and heard it again, "Mr Tumbler, here", behind a dune they could just make out a shape, a small shape lying flat to the ground, they edge cautiously closer, it was the Olive-skinned man, "You all follow me", he got up and ran down the dune, the four followed him, "Do you know this sneaky little Chappy" asked Tony, "Not really" replied Tumbler he has been following us since Rome", they climbed another dune and that's when Tumbler spotted him, the figure was wearing a green and purple kaftan and a mask over his face, "Its time" the figure said putting his hand on Tumblers shoulder, Tumbler looked at the masked face, "Time for what, I don't know what to do" his voice had a slight crackle, "You are the Protector of the Septem child, you know what to do, you just have to dig deep and unleash the power inside you".

"What powers, I've got a few magic rocks, what am I going to do with these?" he held his hand out, the Olive skinned man just closed Tumblers fingers around the Repeater stones and said two words, "Your powerful", Tumbler looked at his hand and just as he was about to ask what the Olive skinned man meant by that he was gone and so was the man in the Green and Purple kaftan.

"Sneaky buggers, aren't they?" remarked Tony, Sledge ignored him and knelt down next to Tumbler, "What do you think the mask is all about?" Tumbler looked at Sledge "He obviously doesn't want to be known but I know the mask, it is the mask of Osirus, the god of Resurrection, the green skin symbolises rebirth but I'm not seeing a link between the current events and this."

"I'm sure it will come to you at some point" said Sledge in a comforting tone "But whilst you mull it over, we better be getting down to that pyramid, anything could happen at any moment and standing around here isn't going to make it any better" and on that note the 4 made their way ever close to the unknown.

Chapter 21

The desert was like a movie set, camera operators from all different news channels were focused on the pyramid, cables ran under their feet off to the vans transmitting the events as they happened and the news reporter filled the air with an array of languages, Italian, Chinese, Brazillian, all trying to get the best shot and the award-winning report.

At times the ground shock but nothing to extreme and Giza just stood there in the dark, it's now Silver walls reflecting the moonlight and blood red from the beams in all direction creating what looked like a laser show, Tumbler actually thought for a brief moment how amazing it looked but was snaped back to reality when he noticed the gold tip of Giza crack slightly.

Tumbler paused for a moment and nudged Carlos who was stood to his left, "Did you see that?", Carlos shrugged "see what?", Tumbler looked again through squinted eyes, "That crack at the top", Carlos narrowed his eyes too "Nope I can't see anything", Tumbler turned to Sledge "Something doesn't feel right, it feels like" but before he could finish the final beam of light at the top of Giza started pulsating and a humming noise emitted from where it met the tip, all the News camera turned and pointed towards the noise and the news reporters fell silent and from nowhere a shockwave rippled down the walls of Giza and across the floor like the aftershock of an explosion, it knocked everyone off their feet and blew all the lenses on the camera's, TV screens worldwide went black and all the reporters dropped their microphones as they buzzed and fizzled out of use, just as the shockwave started to disperse the 4 got to their feet dazed, "What to god damn son of a bitch was that?" Tony shouted, his ears ringing, Tumbler brushed the sand off his shirt, "It must be" but he couldn't finish, another shockwave, this time larger than the last rippled down the walls of the pyramid but this time it was followed by a groaning sound, they looked up and saw the golden tip split into 4 and the pulsating beams plunged deep inside Giza, with this the other 6 beams grew narrower and where pulled inside as if the 7th beam was absorbing all its energy, the silver walls started glowing red like metal being heated in a furnace and then it happened, with an almighty explosion the walls of Giza cracked then shattered into small fragments that were thrown in all direction, the 4 dived to the floor, Tony was caught in the shoulder blade by a shard that was left protruding from his back, he reached over his shoulder and pulled it out, luckily it hadn't gone deep but he still let out a yelp, "Bastard" he grimaced.

The Italian News reporter standing the closest was thrown 30 ft in the air and landed in the sand just yards from Sledge, his body was twitching and blood gurgling from his mouth, Sledge looked closer and saw a silver shard sticking in his forehead and another in his neck, the reporter's eyes were wide open in horror and with a final breath he died.

Sledge fell head first into the sand as shards flew in all direction, one narrowly missing his head and another clipping the top of his right ear leaving a cut that seemed to bleed profusely, he raised his eyes towards his friends, they were nowhere to be seen, he looked back in the direction of where

Giza once stood, all he saw was the dark outline of the Sphinx that was not visible whilst Giza was standing but now stood proud in the dessert moon light, then he noticed the hole, like a meteor had struck leaving a scar on the desserts surface, he crawled his way over and peered over the edge, all he could see was red, the same blood red the beams were before they were sucked inside Giza before it exploded, then he saw them, 2 glowing eyes getting bigger and bigger by the second and just as he thought they had stopped moving they lunged for him, he was frozen and a split second later he felt his body being pulled vigorously out of their way, it was Tony, "Bloody hell that was close", Sledge looked up at the last person he would have expected to save him based on their current relationship status and reluctantly thanked him in his own way, "yeah thanks but I'm sure I could have moved myself", Tony just rolled his eyes and pulled Sledge to his feet, "Your welcome, anyway where did whatever that was go?", Sledge brushed himself off, "I think it went back in the hole, where are Tumbler and Carlos?, "They were in the back of that News van when the explosions occurred so I guess they are still in there", he pointed near a pile of rubble so Sledge made his way to the van with Tony in hot pursuit.

They reached the van and Sledge swung open the doors, Carlos raised a microphone stand above his head in shock, "Shit that was close, I nearly took your head off", Tumbler grabbed the stand and placed it slowly on the floor of the van, "I'm glad you guys are here, evening went crazy when the explosion happened, we had 2 guys trying to force their way in, Carlos had to fight them off, it's like everyone has lost their minds", Sledge looked at him for a second and spoke abnormally slowly, "You have seen what's happened outside haven't you?", Tumbler scratched his head, confused at what his friend was saying, "Well of course I have, that's why we are in here!", Sledge opened the doors further and pointed a the hole where Giza once stood, "No this", Tumbler and Carlos both stepped out of the van and onto the sand, they both looked in the direction of the red, smoking hole in the dessert, they looked at each other, back at the hole and one more time at each other and at the same time had the same response "Holy shit, what's down there?" but before Sledge could answer Tony spoke up, "It looks like Hell down there, something tried grabbing Sledge, if it wasn't for me he would have been a gonna", he slapped Sledge on the back, "I was fine" Sledge replied with anger in his eyes "I didn't need your help", Tony squared up to Sledge, his eyes level with Sledges chin "Oh grow up your prick, for once just accept you can't do everything yourself", Sledge clenched his fist and Tumbler grabbed it before he could swing, "look guys, you both as bad as one another and this is not the time or the place to resolve your differences, we have the lives of billions of people in our hands and acting like 2 kids in a school playground isn't going to save anyone, Sledge and Tony looked at the floor as if they had just been told off by their dads, a few moments passed and they both apologised to Tumbler and all made their way to the edge of the hole.

Tumbler looked over the edge and just as he did he felt a rumble, then another and suddenly the ledge he was standing on gave way, he fell but luckily for him his fall was broken by a ledge, he looked up and saw Sledge reaching into his bag and pulling out a length of rope, "grab the end and ill pull you up", Tumbler reached for the end and wrapped it around his wrist, Tony grabbed the other end and started pulling, just as Sledge was about to grab his hand he heard a whooshing sound coming from the depths of the hole, it got louder like a plane breaking the sound barrier and then he saw them, the same glowing eyes, getting bigger and bigger but this time they were coming at him faster, he shouted at Tony to pull fast and Tumblers arm jolted as the rope picked up speed, he looked below him and saw the eyes heading straight at him and then he felt a bang, like he had been hit by a train, his body was thrown out of the hole and into the air, still attached to the rope, the rope burned through Tony's hands and he had to let go, Tumbler flew into the air and landed on his back next to Carlos, the glowing eyes transformed into a head, followed by an enormous body that slammed onto the ground crushing the Van that was once Tumbler and Carlos's hiding place, the 4 sprinted towards the Sphinx and ducked down behind its massive outstretched feet, the beast thrashed around in the sand trying to get its bearings, a Chinese cameraman stood up in front of it, mesmerised by its eyes and pointed his camera in its direction but before he could press record he was knocked to his feet and engulfed in a ball of fire.

"What in god's name was that" Tony bellowed, he looked at the other 3 who all had their mouths wide open in disbelief and then Tumbler shouted "It's the Fire dragon, Ignis Draco, he has laid dormant all these years, waiting for the moment he would be released into the world, my father told me stories of it when I was young but I never really understood until now, he mentioned the Portal, he mentioned Giza but I didn't put the 2 together", so what does this mean Sledge asked Tumbler in a panic but Tumbler was in a daze, as if he was having an out of body experience and he just kept repeating the same phrase "From the sands of the dessert he shall rise and we shall fall bringing the end of the earth and the beginning of a new dawn, the dawn of fire, the uprising of the 7 beasts of the Septem".

Tony looked at him "Oh that explains everything" he said sarcastically, but before he could continue Sledge grabbed Tumbler and shook him, Tumblers eyes opened and peered back into Sledges big blue eyes, he felt safe for a moment before reality kicked back in, "What do you mean the uprising of the 7 beasts of Septem, do you mean we have to kill them again", Tumbler looked at the floor, "kind of" he muttered, "What the fuck do you mean kind of?" Sledges voice boomed, "Well those were just the little ones, I thought we would stop Annakus before she got to the seventh location, I never thought it would go this far but it has and now things are flooding back, I must have switched my brain off hoping it would never come to this, why me, why does it have to happen to me?".

Sledge shook him again "Well shit has just got really real now, so you are telling me it's not just the Fire dragon, it's the other 7 creatures too, Shenlong, the Aluxs, I thought something was off when I saw them on the news when we are on the plane" but before he could finish he saw Ignis Draco, the Fire dragon launch himself into the air above the hole and hover, then his mouth opened and what sounded like all the lions in the world roaring at the same time emitted from his fiery mouth followed by a series of clicks, they covered their ears to block out the noise, Tony moved away and pulled out his phone, he had a signal and surprisingly to him he also had 4G, he muttered to himself "I can get a 4g signal in the middle of the dessert during a worldwide disaster but not when I'm stood in an airplane hangar in the middle of an airport" he giggled to himself for a moment and pressed the News app on the screen, "boys you may want to see this", he turned the screen to the other 3 and they watched in astonishment, "The BBC news reporter spoke slowly, "We are getting reports that all Seven wonders of the world are gone, replaced by large craters containing a red mist, wait, we are getting a live feed from Brazil", the screen switched to an Brazilian news reported "Christ is gone, its looks like Hell has taken our lord", the camera zoomed in to where Christ the Redeemer once stood, arms no longer spread, just a hole spewing red mist and then they saw her, Biotata raised her serpent head and slide down the mountain side, destroying everything in her path, Carlos fell to his knees as he saw the town he called home flattened by her massive body, the screams of his fellow Brazilians echoed through the phones speakers, he turned away and sobbed.

"It's happening everywhere" Tumbler stood up and pulled Carlos to his feet, "The Fire Dragon is the key, we need to stop him before they lay waste to the entire world," Suddenly he saw two figures emerge from the darkness, the man in the green mask closely followed by the Olive-skinned man.

Chapter 22

They all huddled together but their discussions were halted by screams, screams of terror rang out from the nearby city of Cairo, Ignis Draco bellowing out streams of fire onto the city below, its large wings creating a wind like no other, toppling buildings, market stalls lifted into the air scattering the traders in all directions, the city was falling, alight in flames like the sun had fallen from the sky, people ran in all directions, burning, grabbing loved ones and pulling them into any area that looked remotely safe but to no avail as the Fire Dragon bellowed more flames, Cairo looked like the centre of Hells itself.

They flicked back to Tony's phone for a brief second to review the breaking news as it happened, the report flicking constantly between all seven locations, it was carnage, the death toll was rising by the second, one million, two million, it did not stop.

The man in the green mask turned to Tumbler, "You have to stop this now, you know you can, you need to look deep into yourself, unleash the power of the protectors, it's in your blood my child, your father had it but you are stronger", Tumbler looked at the man in the Green mask, his green and purple kaftan blowing in the wind, "You knew my father?" he said in a surprised voice but there was no time for an answer, The man in the Green mask reached into his pocket and pulled out 2 small marbles, they looked similar to the ones Tumbler had used against Shenlong back at the Great wall but these seemed to pulsate in the man's hand, Tumbler couldn't figure out where he had got them from, this guy was full of surprises but there were more important things to worry about, the man raised his hand and threw them in the direction of the Fire Dragon, they hovered for a moment and then shot off towards the burning city and just as they were a few hundred feet from the dragon they exploded into a massive ball of multi-coloured light, Ignis Dracos head turned towards the light and his eyes fixed on the man in the Green mask, he swung his tail knocking the top off a nearby building and flew in the direction of the source of the lights, he was there in seconds, the group threw themselves down the dune and rolled in all directions avoiding the fire balls being thrown at them, Carlos landed on Tumbler, Sledge grabbed his bag and threw a knife in Tony's direction, "Used one of these before?" he asked Tony sarcastically, "More times than you can imagine" replied Tony as he tucked the blade into his belt and headed towards the crater.

The Fire Dragon launched himself towards the Man in the Green mask, Tumbler ran towards him but the man waved him away, he shouted at Tumbler, "You prepare yourself, Ill create a distraction, you are the only one who can stop this", Tumbler turned and ran towards Sledge and Tony then he heard something smash into the sand where he had been standing not minutes before, a fire ball hit the sand between him and the Man in the green mask causing so much heat it turned the sand into glass, shards protruded from the dessert floor and then he saw blood, he checked himself but it wasn't his and then he heard a name, a name he was familiar with but not one he had heard for years, "Asim no".

He looked in the direction the name was being called from, he saw the olive-skinned man kneeling over the man in the green mask, Tumbler turned on his heels and ran back towards the pair, the olive skinned man was cradling the Green masked man's head, tears where running down his face, the Fire Dragon hovered above them, eyes burning, Tumbler looked at him, anger took over every part of his body, he reached into his pocket and pulled out a repeater stone and threw it at the dragon, it exploded in all directions causing Ignis Draco to pull back for a brief moment, the Man in the green mask opened his mouth and he spoke two words clearly "Clypeus stone", Tumbler reached into his other pocket and pulled out the stone, he rolled it in his hand and suddenly a blue light shot out from the top, it broke off into 4 and the light arched its way back to the ground creating a blue shield around the 3 of them, The Fire Dragon launched a fire ball at them just as the 4 points hit the ground and ricochet off the shield, the olive skinned man wiped a tear from his cheek, "The shield will only last 5 minutes" he turned his attention back to the man in the Green mask, "Asim can you hear me", there was no response, Tumbler looked at the olive skinned man "Asim was my Great grandfathers name", the olive-skinned man put his hand on the mask and slowly removed it revealing the face of a man that looked old and weathered, the face of a man that had lived a very long life, "it is your great Grandfather", Tumbler was speechless.

"But how is this possible?" exclaimed Tumbler in bemusement, "My father told me he died in the Mexican American war in 1849", the Olive-skinned man wiped Asim's brow with the sleeve of his shirt and continued to explain whilst the Fire dragon continued throwing fire balls at the shield.

"Your Great grandfather did die in 1849, I had visited his grave numerous times after his death to pay respects to the First Protector of the Septem, Tumbler looked at him in amazement, "But how do you know about the Septem, I was always told we were the only ones to know", the Olive-skinned man continued to explain, "I am the last surviving member of the Order of the Septem, 7 men given the duty to protect each one of the seven wonders of the world from the likes of Annakus in the event the 7 pieces were stolen it was our duty to defend the exact location, the keyhole of the piece, when Annakus found out you had settled in Scotland she visited each location and wiped us out one by one so we wouldn't cause a threat when she did get her hands on the Pieces, which obviously she did, I fled Petra once I knew what was happening and the only person I knew could help was Asim but he was dead".

"But how did you bring him back after all this time?" Tumblers mind was all over the place at this point, the Olive-skinned man continued "I knew about the mask of Osirus, the god of resurrection as it was knowledge only given to the Order of the Septem, I took the mask to your Great Grandfathers crypt and placed it on his body, it bought him back, the reason his skin is green is because it symbolises rebirth, we then tracked you since locating you in Mexico and have been following you ever since".

Tumbler had question after question running through his mind and wanted to ask them all at once but before he could Asim opened his eyes and forced out a sentence "There is an eighth piece" he gasped for breath, Tumbler and the Olive-skinned man looked at each other, "What do you mean Asim, an 8th piece, but how?" the Olive skinned man seemed confused, Asim another deep breath and gestured to Tumbler to come closer, Tumbler moved his ear to Asim's mouth and struggled to make out the word, suddenly Asim's face distorted in pain, he squeezed the Olive-skinned man's hand and with one final, gurgling breath he passed away, Tumbler looked at the Olive-skinned man who was trembling with grief, "Asim, come back to us", he put the mask back on but nothing happened, he tried several times but to no avail, he placed the mask on the sand and closed Asim's eyes, he was gone.

He turned to Tumbler, "What did he say to you?", Tumbler was in shock, he had always wondered what his Great Grandfather would have been like and he was both happy that he had met him even if it was only for 5 minutes but filled with anger because he had been taken from him so quickly, Tumbler felt rage building inside him for the first time, he looked at the Olive-skinned man with piercing eyes, "What did he say?" the Olive-skinned man repeated just as the shield collapsed around them, Tumbler looked back at him for a brief second and before running out into the desert he replied through gritted teeth, "Never rest"

The olive-skinned man was confused, there is an eighth piece, Never rest, none of it made sense but there was no time to ponder, by this time Tony and Sledge joined the pair as they faced up at the Fire dragon, beating his wings so hard it was a struggle for them to stand, sand was blowing in their eyes making it difficult to see, another fire ball landed within feet of Sledge causing him to fall into Tony, "Hey watch it big guy" Tony exclaimed, Sledge looked at Tumbler, "What's the plan", Tumbler was shaking with anger, his fists clenched so tight his hands had gone white, "You and Tony distract him whilst myself and Carlos go round the back, where is Carlos anyway?", Tony looked up for a moment, "He disappeared over the dune earlier, said there was something he needed to do", Tumbler thought for a moment then his face changed, he looked at Sledge "Annakus, he is going to find Annakus, he is on a revenge mission", Sledge looked at Tumbler, "We have more important things to worry about at the moment" pointing at the Fire Dragon "let him do his thing".

Chapter 23

Annakus watched from a distance as The Fire Dragon laid waste to everything in sight, she laughed a maniacal laugh that echoed across the desert, "I've done it, now who's powerful father", she rubbed her bony hands together and turned away for a brief moment, suddenly she felt a thud as she was knocked clean off he feet and rolled down the dune, something or someone was on top of her, pinning her to the ground, she could only make out a shadow in the moon light but she heard the voice clearly, "This is for Jose" as a fist slammed into her jaw dazing her for a brief second, then another on the other side of her face, she raised her hands and forced her foot into the shadows stomach, the shadow gasped and loosened their grip, the light from the fires below lit up the shadows face, it was Carlos.

Annakus got to her feet, blood dripping from a wound on her chin where Carlos had struck her the second time, Carlos lunged for her once more but this time she moved and he fell down the dune, he picked himself up and ran for her again but Annakus was ready, she pulled a small knife from her boot and grasp it tight in her left hand, Carlos jumped at her and just as he was close enough she struck catching him in the rib cage just below his right lung, his eyes widened in pain and he put his hand over the wound to stem the blood, she struck again but this time on his left side puncturing his lung, he gasp for breath and fell to his knees, Annakus slowly grabbed his hair and pulled his head back exposing his throat, "Good try but it's time to visit your brother" and with that she ran the blade across his throat, Carlos gurgled, the blood looked black in the moon light, she let go of his hair and he fell on is back, Annakus put her foot on his shoulder and pushed as hard as she could, Carlos rolled down the dune and came to rest in the darkness, he gasped one last time and with his final breath forced out "You will die before the night is out", and he was gone, she looked at him with no remorse "That's what you think" and made her way into the chaos.

Unaware of what had just happened, the remaining three carried out their plan minus Carlos, Sledge and Tony sprinted behind The Fire Dragon, dodging left and right to avoid its thrashing tail, Sledge reached into his bag and pulled out a bowie knife and threw it as hard as he could, it bounced off Ignis Dracos scales landing back at Sledges feet, Tony grinned "That went well guvnor" and tried himself, this time the knife stuck between the scales and Ignis Draco moved his head in the direction of the pair throwing a stream of fire at their feet, they looked for Tumbler and could see him standing with his head down and his fists still clenched.

Tumbler gritted his teeth and held his breath, the rage built up more and more in his belly, he felt something he had never felt before, a roaring through his whole body, a pulsating throb from his toes to the top of his head that ran back down both his arms and then it happened, his arms shot out in front of him and from his fingertips he emitted a shockwave followed by a bright blue light that knocked The Fire Dragon from its hovering location above the red mist of the crater, it crashed into the Sphinx directly behind it causing the head of the Sphinx to crumble under the weight, the Fire Dragon shook itself and beat its large wings lifting him back into the air and back towards the crater, clicking and roaring coming from its mouth, Tumbler could feel a second wave pulsing through his body but before he could do anything he was knocked to the ground, "No" screamed Annakus as she threw herself at him, they both rolled towards the crater, the red mist being blown by the beating of the Fire Dragons large red wings, they tussled in the sand, each trying to overpower the other, Tumbler managed to break free of her grasp and waved over to Sledge and Tony for assistance, the pair came running to his aid but were thrown back by another large stream of fire from Ignis Draco, they looked on helplessly as Annakus took a second strike in Tumblers direction but this time Tumbler was too quick, he stepped to one side and Annukus slipped, losing her balance and falling towards the edge of the crater, she held on with long, black fingers, clawing at the sand to grip to something remotely stable, she swung the leather bag with the 7 on the front that had contained the Wonder pieces over her head and it caught on a shard left over from the initial explosion from Giza, it held, Tumbler edged towards the crater, the strap was slowly ripping under the weight of Annakus, he looked her in the eyes and for the first time he saw fear "I should let you die for what you have done, you have killed millions and for what, to prove a point to a man who has died", Annakus looked up at him "He died a long time ago, this is for me now", Tumbler felt that anger building again "He died 20 minutes ago, he saw what you have done and he died disappointed in his daughter and her actions", Annakus looked at him bewildered, the strap ripped some more and she dropped some more.

The Fire Dragon looped around the crater before noise diving towards Tumbler, he jumped and rolled and lay on his back,

The fire Dragon swooped into the air and made another attempt but this time Tumbler was ready, his body pulsed and another shockwave emitted from his fingers but this time the blue light cut through the dragons left wing causing it to spiral towards the ground, the ground shook as it hit knocking every one of their feet, the strap of the bag snapped and Annakus fell then suddenly she stopped, Tumbler had grabbed her hand "If I let you die then I'm no better than you" he snarled at her then he heard Sledges voice "Tumbler move" but it was too late, the Fire Dragon got to its feet and bound towards Tumbler, with his free hand Tumbler aimed at the speeding Dragons foot and emitted a second smaller shockwave but this time the blue beam severed its right leg, it toppled towards the crater, the edge crumbled and it fell into the depths of the red mist, the crater started to shake and began to close over, Tumbler slipped into the mist still holding onto Annakus but the shaking caused Annakus to lose her grip, Tumbler grabbed the bag strap and she stopped falling for a moment but Tumbler kept moving, just as he thought that was it he felt a hand around his wrist, it was Sledge, "let go of the strap, I can't hold you both", "I can't" shouted Tumbler, "You must!" bellowed Sledge "I can't save you both", Tumbler looked at Annakus and let go of the strap, she plummeted deep into the hole screaming as she fell "The world is no more".

The crater grew smaller, Sledge slid across the sand still holding onto Tumbler who still had the empty bag swinging from his hand, suddenly there was a jolt on Tumblers foot, somehow Annakus had fallen onto the ledge Tumbler had landed on earlier and was clawing her way up Tumblers leg, from the depths they heard a roar, Sledge saw the outliner of The Fire Dragon dragging itself up the wall of the crater with its good remaining wing and leg, it opened its mouth and bit down on Annakus's foot, she screamed, then the Fire dragon lost its footings and fell back pulling Annakus with it, Sledge winced as he shoulder jolted under the weight, Tumbler swung the bag up to Sledge who grabbed onto it but the weight was too much to bear, Tumbler looked up at him with his big brown eyes "Thank you" he said to Sledge and he let go of his hand, Sledge watched as Tumbler and Annakus fell, "No Tumbler, No" screamed Sledge and just before Tumbler disappeared into the red mist he shouted what sounded like "Never rest", Sledge slumped in the sand, bag still in his hand, his friend and travelling companion was gone and with that the crater closed over and everything went dark.

Chapter 24

Sledge lay in the sand for what felt like an eternity, he stared into the starry sky, a tear ran down his cheek and is body felt numb, he hadn't known Tumbler for long but felt like he had just lost a brother, he closed his eyes but all he could see was his friend falling into the red mist, his last words running through Sledges mind like it was playing on a loop "Never rest, Never rest", what did he mean, it was over, Annakus was gone, the crater had closed over and the Fire dragon was defeated, why did he have to go on, he couldn't find the answer, minutes past and Sledge heard shuffling in the sand behind him, he sat up and wiped the tears from his face, he turned and saw Tony standing over him, shirt ripped and blood on his forehead.

"What happened to you?" Sledges asked Tony, Tony wiped his forehead with his sleeve and looked at the blood stain "Oh its just a nick, damn Fire dragon thingy clipped me with its claw, nearly took my head off but I've had worse, we better find the others and get out of here", Sledge stood up and looked at Tony, We are the others, no one else left but us", Tony was confused "But where is Tumbler and Carlos?", Sledges voice crackled but he held back his emotions "He's gone", Tony was taken back "What do you mean gone, gone as in gone already and we are following him later or gone as in gone, gone?", "Gone as in gone, gone" Sledge replied "He sacrificed himself to save us all and when I say us all I mean the world, he took Annakus with him, that's his 2 greatest successes".

Tony forced his arm around Sledges shoulder and patted it manly, "look mate, we have had our differences but lets put them to one side for his sake, he was a great guy and had a lot to carry for a small guy, he did what he was destined to do and let's remember him for it", Sledge nodded and brushed Tony's hand off his shoulder, for a second Tony thought all he had said had gone in one ear and out the other but from nowhere Sledge grabbed his hand and shook it violently "You're a good guy Tony, bit of a knob sometimes but a good guy none the less", Tony laughed "I'll take that, what about Carlos", Sledge hadn't seen him since he disappeared, "Well I guess he found Annakus but on the basis that Annakus came back and he didn't then I assume he may be dead too", Tony shook his head.

The pair sat on the sand and Tony pulled out his phone, the battery was on 15% and his signal was blinking in and out of reception, he raised it above his head and the 4G signal pinged up in the corner, he clicked his News app and the two watched the live stream, it cut to a British news reporter stood in the ruins of Machu Picchu, Tony turned the volume up so they could her what she was saying, the reporter looked at the camera "It's been chaos here for the last 2 hours, thousands of tourists have lost their lives and many more are injured but wait something is happening", the camera shook, she turned her back to the camera then flung her arm around and forced the camera into the direction of the crater that had appeared 2 hours before "Its closing over, its like a giant vacuum is pulling the red mist in and the unknown creature that killed hundreds is being dragged in with it, in all my years of reporting I have never seen anything like this", the cameraman hands where shaking and he zoomed in on the blurry figure of Pishtay clawing at the ground trying its hardest not to be dragged in the closing hole, the News reader at the studio interrupted the report "I'm going to have to stop you Kelly, we are getting news from the other locations" he cut to a split screen live feed showing the ruins of the Colosseum, the Taj mahal, The great wall and Chichen Itza, all showing the same scene of the craters closing in and the creatures being dragged back into the closing holes, the pair watched as an Alux flew past the camera as if it was stuck in a whirlwind and just as it was about to be sucked into the depths of the crater it grabbed a rucksack left by one of the dead and it vanished, the flailing body of Shenlong took out the Chinese news reporter and his van as it was pulled into the depth of the hole along with tons of debris left over from the collapsed section of the great wall, then a messaged flashed up at the bottom of the screen, it read "Nearly 200 million deaths recorded worldwide, 150 million across the 8 locations of the craters and another estimated 50 million from disasters caused by the events in cities around the world", The News reader shuffled his papers and continued to read the news "I'm being told that the combined energy caused by all 8 craters opening at once caused earthquakes that were felt all over the world as far as London and Australia, our sympathies go out to all those who have lost someone or are still awaiting news".

Tony switched off his phone to preserve the remaining 8% battery, "unbloody believable, one woman caused all this, it will take years to rebuild, the world has lost some amazing, historic sites and for what, nothing that's what, lets get home, I can't take any more of this".

Sledge stood and looked at the last place he had seen his friend, he turned to Tony "Give me a minute", he walked over and pulled out of his bag the Knife he had forged back at Chichen Itza, he stabbed it into the sand and closed his eyes "Tumbler if you can hear me I want to say you made your father proud, you were a great man and travelling alongside you was an honour, I never had a brother but that day back in Killington I felt I had found one, be safe Brother and say hi to your dad for me, until we meet again" he kissed his fingers and tapped them on the top of the knifes pummel, he turned and made his way back to Tony who lit up a cigarette, "Want one" he waved the pack at Sledge, "No thanks but I need drink" Tony grinned, brushed his hair out of his eyes and they made their way across the silent desert.

Chapter 25

The sun was starting to rise on the horizon, Sledge and Tony had been walking for 2 hours before they came across an abandoned car, its drivers door was open, the previous owners bag still in the back seat and they keys still hanging in the ignition, Tony went through the bag and threw Sledge a bottle of water, "here you go, there is only 1 bottle so don't neck it all" Sledge took a swig and threw it back to Tony, the pair got in the car and Tony turned the keys, nothing, he tried again and this time it spluttered into life, the fuel gage showed 20 miles of range in the tank "Perfect" said Tony "If I'm right and I normally am it is approximately 11 miles to Cairo airport, if this thing makes it then hopefully there will be a plane and I can take you back to Scotland.

Sledge threw his bag in the back seat on top of the other bag and put Tumblers old Satchel with the seven on the front down by his feet, "Lets go then, I've had enough of all this sand," Tony put the car into gear and wheel spun back onto the road.

It only took them 10 minutes to drive to Cairo airport but they were both glad to be sat down for a while after the events of the past 24 hrs, they left the car in the arrivals parking and climbed a fence into the airport, the planes were scattered over the runway but none were in any state to fly, Tony pulled open the door to a large hanger and spotted a small Cirrus SF50 Vision Jet, "That will do nicely" he was grinning from ear to ear like a small child on Christmas morning, they climbed into the jet but then his face changed from ecstatic to disappointment "The bloody instrument panel isn't working, all the wires are hanging out" Sledge looked at him and smiled "You're the engineer, surely you can rewire it in no time", Tony looked at the wires for a few moments and then turned back to Sledge, "Grab me a tool kit", Sledge stepped off the plane and searched the hanger and found a rusty old tool box on a bench in the corner, he climbed back onto the plane and place it at Tony's feet, "I'll wait here" and he slumped down in one of the plush black leather seats and took a drink out of a bottle of whiskey he found in one of the compartments.

30 minutes past with the air being filled with constant profanities and then the instrument panel lit up, "Yes" Tony shouted, "Give me some of that Whiskey", Sledge threw him the half empty bottle and tony drank what was left, he threw the empty bottle on the floor and cranked up the engine, the jet screamed into life, "Buckle up" shouted Tony as he put the headphones on, "London here we come" he taxied out of the hanger and pulled back the controls and made their way back.

They had been flying for just under 5 hours when they started to make their descent, Sledge looked out of the window and below he could see large cracks in the earth, small fires blazed from what looked like upturned cars, he grabbed his bag and pushed Tumblers satchel into it closing the zip and swinging it onto his back, he sat in the seat next to Tony who was focused on the ground ahead, a few moments of silence past and then Tony flicked the switch to drop the landing wheels, he pulled up on the controls and the tyres touched down on the tarmac at Inverness Airport and the sound of rubber screeched as the Cirrus SF50 came to a holt, Tony unclipped his seat belt and opened the door, it had been raining and the ground was wet but Sledge was pleased to be nearing the end of his journey, "How far have you got to go from here" asked Tony "Well Killington is only about 10 miles from Inverness so the walk will be nice, clear my head", Tony slapped him on the back "Stay in touch me old mucker, maybe I can come and visit one day or maybe our paths will cross again ,you never know" he winked at Sledge who winked back sarcastically "Not for a long time I hope, what will you do now?" replied Sledge swinging the bag onto his right shoulder, "I'll probably head back to Bethnal Green, see if the old gaff is still standing and go from there", with that Tony pulled the door on the jet closed and sat back in the pilots seat, he put on the headphones and saluted at Sledge before starting the engine back up and pulling the plane into the air, Sledge turned and started his walk back to Killington.

It was only a short flight back to London and Tony landed safely at London Gatwick, he looked at the airport, its had taken some damage, he stood in the doorway for a brief moment and sniffed the air "Hello girl, it's nice to be home, and still wearing the old lady London's perfume, I've not smelt that for years", he took in his surroundings, found an old motorbike in the departures car park and sped off into the distance bound for Bethnal green and his old stomping grounds.

Chapter 26

It was nearing 9:30pm by the time Sledge made his way past the "Welcome to Killington" sign, he stopped for a moment and took in the flickering lights of the town ahead of him, the smell of the countryside and the sound of the birds making their way to their roasts was amazing, he took in the silence, took in a big deep breath of fresh air and made his way down the road.

It took another 10 minutes for Sledge to reach his workshop, he dropped his bag by his feet and gazed at his front door, he closed his eyes and pictured his own bed, the bottle of whiskey he had for emergencies hidden inside the barrel in the corner and sighed, he reached above the door frame and slide his hand left and right until he felt the key and pushed it into the keyhole and turned, the door cracked open and a puff of dust creeped up his nose causing him to sneeze, the light in the house across the road flicked on and one of the residents opened his bedroom window and simply shouted "Evening Sledge" as if Sledge hadn't even left, Sledge picked up his bag and closed the door behind him.

The forge was ice cold, and the workshop was silent, the first time Sledge had really heard nothing at all for weeks, he slumped on the bed still fully clothed and slept like a baby.

Morning came and the sun shone through the dusty window right onto Sledges face, he stretched his arms and yawned, he threw back the covers and made his way to the kitchen and lit the wood burner, he filled his kettle with water and put it on top of the burner and went to his fridge, he picked up the milk, it was heavy, he twisted off the lid and sniffed and then threw it in the sink, it was like yogurt, "I'll have a black coffee" he thought to himself and went over to the cupboard, he pulled the top off the coffee pot and a small mouse jumped out, Sledge dropped the coffee pot spilling the coffee granules all over the floor, the mouse scurried off under the door, "Shit" cried Sledge, then he remembered he had picked up some sachets of coffee from the hotel back in Rome, he rummaged through his bag and ripped open all 3 and poured them into his mug.

Sledge pulled out Tumblers satchel and hung it on a rusty nail next to the door, the kettle whistled and he poured the hot water into his mug and slumped into his big, dirty arm chair, he looked at the satchel by the door, suddenly there was a knock at the door, he put down his mug and walked over to the door, as he opened it he saw a small figure in a heavy overcoat, the hood was pulled up, "Tumbler?" Sledge boomed, the figure turned round and looked up at Sledge "Hello" said the figure and pulled down the hood, "oh its only you Mrs Gillatt", she looked at him for a minute "Well that's a lovely welcome to the lady who used to sneak you cakes through my window on the way to school" she grinned and gave him a huge hug "Welcome back my boy, tell me about your trip", Sledge smiled "How long have you got?" he enquired, Mrs Gillatt looked at him with her small brown eyes, "For you, all the time in the world" and Sledge poured her a mug of coffee and began his unbelievable story.

Hours past and Mrs Gillatt could not believe what she had just heard, she did not have a TV and the radio she had was broken but she told Sledge how she had heard stories and rumours going around the town about the small man and the big Scotsman that saved the world, Sledge smiled a quirky smile "it definitely wasn't as glamourous as they have made it out to be", Mrs Gillatt put her empty mug on the edge of the table and brushed off her coat "I better get going, Mr Gillatt is going to wonder where I have been" She pulled Sledge down to her level and gave him a kiss on the cheek and whispered in his ear "Just remember you still have to take Rosemary out for that drink you promised her 6 months ago" she winked at him and pulled the door closed behind her.

Weeks passed and Sledges life was beginning to get back to a bit of normality, there had been no reporters knocking on his door for a week now and he could get back to what he loved the most, forging knives, he had an order from the local butcher for a new cleaver and it was just getting to the point he could quench it, he pulled it out of the forge and swung it back and forth until the metal was glowing a nice salmon colour and plunged it into the oil, he listened for any pings or cracks but none came, he wiped the cleaver off and put it down on the anvil to cool, he picked up a glass off a pile of magazines and knocked back some of the whiskey, he put the glass back down on the magazine and grabbed some wood for the handle, he picked the glass up again to finish off the remaining whiskey but knocked the pile of magazines onto the floor, they scattered and one of them fell open on an article about Everest, he glanced at it for a moment and an image of Tumbler popped into his head, his voice echoing his final words "Never rest", Sledge thought nothing of it and picked up the magazines and placed them back on the table.

Suddenly there was a knock on the door, "Not another bloody reporter" he thought to himself and swung open the door, "look I've told you everything" but before he could finish his mouth dropped open in amazement, standing in front of him was the Olive-skinned man, Sledge couldn't believe his eyes "What the hell are you doing here", the Olive skinned man pushed past Sledge in a hurry, "Sit, Sit" he said in a rushed tone "I know what it means, I know where the eighth piece is".

Sledge pulled up a chair and watched the Olive-skinned man pace backwards and forwards saying nothing, 10 minutes past and Sledge was losing his patience, "Are you going to tell me or what? And what are you going on about an eighth piece? Tumbler only ever mentioned 7 pieces, 7 pieces, 7 Wonders" said Sledge confused, the Olive skinned man looked at Sledge and took a deep breath "Tumbler didn't say Never rest he said Everest, Asim told him about the eighth piece just before he died, Tumbler never got chance to tell you" Sledge couldn't believe it, he looked at the olive skinned man "that is so weird, just before you came in I knocked a magazine on the floor and it opened on an article about Everest, he handed the Olive skinned man the magazine and he flicked through the pages, he stared at the 2 page spread, words covering the photo of the highest mountain in the world and pointed at the peak, "It's inside" whispered the Olive skinned man to Sledge, Sledge took the magazine and looked at it for a moment, "I think I know what is coming next", he rolled his eyes and the Olive skinned man just looked straight back at him and with a soft, slightly nervous voice he replied "We must go".

Sledge slide into his chair, he looked around the workshop then sat bolt upright and stormed towards the door, the Olive skinned man was taken back by the sudden movement of this huge man he didn't really know, Sledge grabbed Tumblers satchel off the hook and dropped it onto the table and as he did the flap opened and a small pouch dropped onto the floor, he picked it up and poured the contents into his hand, he looked closely, there was 1 Iter stone, 1 Clypeus stone and 1 Repeater stone and something else that Sledge hadn't seen before, he focused in on the object, it was square and gold in colour, neither knew what it was, Sledge put the stones back in the pouch and put the pouch in the pocket of the satchel, as he does this he notices the corner of a piece of paper tucked into the seam of the bag, he pulls it out, unfolds it and reads it to himself, it read:

"To whom may find this letter, the world is ever changing and with this your life may change too, each day is different and every corner has a new beginning, each step takes you further into your journey than you could ever imagine and with every new step life changes with it, embrace the good and the bad, use it to grow and become the person you never thought you could become, life is there for changing, life is there to enjoy and each day writes a new story, stories are to be told, to bring joy to those around you, to inspire others to change their lives and for each and every person in the world to live a wholesome life, as you read this letter your life may be about to change, grasp it with both hands and embark on a journey that will change your life forever, write your own story, your companion ,Asim".

Sledge folded the paper up and tucked it back inside the seam of the bag, the Olive skinned man looked at Sledge, "What did it say?" but Sledge didn't reply, he knew how close the Olive skinned man had been to Asim and now wasn't the time to tell him, with this in mind he turned and put two knives into the satchel and grabbed his holdall that still had some bits in that he had packed before he had left with Tumbler, he felt an air of déjà vu, he looked up and for a moment thought it was Tumbler standing in front of him until the Olive Skinned man spoke "You better pack coat and boots" he pointed at the old sheep skinned coat and lined boots in the corner "It get very cold", Sledge looked at the photo of the snow covered mountain, "So where do we start" he asked the Olive skinned man as he blew out the candle on the table putting the workshop into near darkness.

The pair stepped outside and Sledge locked the door, they made their way to the outskirts of Killington and stopped by the sign reading "Thank you for driving carefully through our town" the letters that made up Killington on the sign sparkled in the moon light and Sledge looked back at the flickering lights of the town he thought he would never leave again, he sighed and stared at the stars, "where first?" he eventually asked the Olive skinned man, "We need to get to Nepal, we need to find a plane", Sledge looked at the Olive skinned man with a smile "London, I know just the man" and with that the pair disappeared into the darkness, about to embark on a journey that could change their lives for better or worse.

Printed in Great Britain
by Amazon